Beth Heywood
2008

Dive into a good book at
www.swimmingkangaroo.com

This page is here to make the page count work out.

Cherished
Swimming Kangaroo Books, May 2008

Swimming Kangaroo Books
Arlington, Texas
ISBN: Paperback 978-1-934041-59-8
Other Available formats: PDF, HTML, Mobi (No ISBN's are assigned)

LCCN: 2007942561
British Library Cataloguing in Publication Data.
A catalogue record for this book is available from the British Library.

 This book is a work of fiction and any resemblance to persons, living or dead, or events is purely coincidental. They are productions of the author's imagination and used fictitiously.

Cover art by Skylar Sinclair

This page is here to make the page count work out.

Cherished

by

Beth Heywood

Swimming Kangaroo Books Arlington, Texas

This page is here to make the page count work out.

Acknowledgements

For Dindy and Jess, many thanks for your help, encouragement, and suggestions.

For Errol, my husband, my lover, my best friend,
and also for Greg, Benia, Maria, and Lucas and Howard,
Madison, and Derrilynn.

PROLOGUE

April 2, 1946 Augustus Island, South Atlantic Ocean.

The new day dawned bright and clear with a freshening wind from the southwest that brought the fish to their feeding grounds. On shore women cooked hot breakfasts on wood stoves for their husbands and children, while on the water men and their sons hauled in their fishing nets and started to head for home with their catch. It would be a busy day just like any other for the small island community.

Hundreds of fathoms below the ocean's surface, unnoticed and unremarked by anyone or anything except for shoals of exotic colored fish, the tectonic plates shifted slightly. Sufficient enough to cause a groan of resistance from the seabed, but not strong enough to cause a ripple on the water's surface.

CHAPTER ONE

Adelaide Rawtenstall was frightened. More frightened than she'd ever been in all her eighteen years.

For the thousandth time she checked her watch. Five-fifty. Just over four hours before the ship was due to sail.

The line of embarking passengers in front of her shuffled slowly, oh so slowly as they showed their tickets, embraced friends and relatives in long drawn-out farewells and finally boarded the SS *Neptune.*

Adelaide was fearful she'd never make it to the ship, that someone might recognize her, prevent her from leaving.

She glanced around her, recognizing no one. That was good. But it didn't mean she was safe. She wouldn't be safe until she was on board the SS *Neptune* and sailing out of British waters.

Even then, she doubted she'd ever feel properly safe again. Her father-in-law, James Rawtenstall, was an obsessed and ruthless man, with a long arm of influence that stretched across the hills and rivers of Northern England.

Unconsciously, she hugged the bundle she carried closer to her chest and smiled lovingly at the sleeping baby with rosy cheeks and wavy black hair. 'Almost there, Daniel,' she whispered, 'then we'll be fine. We'll stay hidden in our cabin, as snug as two bugs in a rug, all the way to Augustus Island.'

Slowly the line of embarking passengers in front of her shuffled forward along the tarmac. Please hurry, she thought. Am I the only person here with any sense of urgency?

She snuggled her sleeping, infant son nearer, trying not to transmit her fears to him. For all that he was tiny, Daniel had powerful lungs, and if he started to scream all eyes would be upon her.

The line inched forward like nonchalant snails in no hurry at all to reach a funeral pyre, while Adelaide felt her very life was at stake.

Around her the April air was crisp and chilly, as only an April spring morning can be. She breathed in the dawn. And hope. Overhead, gulls squalled and circled, cajoling the dawn to hurry and deliver a day of promise after the bleakest of all winters.

Adelaide tried to maintain an air of calm. In her grey, nondescript clothes no-one paid her any attention, which was exactly what she wanted.

Suddenly it was her turn to board. This was it. The final leaving of home as she knew it. Sadness and anticipation thrilled through her. Goodbye to her feelings of terror, hello to a new life and the safety it would hold for them both.

She put her hand inside her old leather handbag —a gift from her late grandmother —and pulled out her boarding pass.

'Augustus Island, eh?' remarked the young sailor. 'In the South we call it Damnation Island. Very few people leave there.'

A sliver of apprehension sliced through Adelaide. The information she'd been given about Augustus Island was different. She'd heard it was a place of wild beauty, maybe not so dissimilar to the moors at home, where in the summer for a few pence she could hire a horse, ride it bareback across the heathers, hear the horses hooves pounding the turf beneath her, feel the wind whip through her hair, raising it like a curtain behind her, before letting it drop heavily against her shoulders. And in the winter she could walk across the moorland tracks and listen to the eerie shrieks and cries of the birds in the mists.

She met the young sailor's gaze steadily. 'I don't intend to leave.'

And she didn't. She intended to stay for at least eighteen years.

Until her son was grown up and James Rawtenstall had had

time to cool his heels and mellow.

Eighteen years.

'That's all right then, ain't it, Miss? Too many mail order brides go there and get all homesick. They have a devil of a job getting home again.'

'I'm not a mail order bride,' Adelaide lied crisply. 'I'm a widow.'

'My condolences, ma'am.' Deep, caressing, the words rolled around the new-comer's mouth like cannon-balls coming to fire.

Adelaide turned at the unexpected voice behind her, taking in the handsome form, the blond Saxon masculinity. The masculinity of sea-farers from ages past.

'I'm Luke Collins. It's my job to show you to your cabin. What's your name, please, ma'am?'

'Margaret Aspinall.' She lied again, praying Mum would forgive her for using her name.

Luke Collins scrutinized the slight figure before him, his eyes making a quick sweep of her from head to toe. Her hair was pulled back behind her head and almost hidden by a scarf. What was visible was as black and shiny as a raven's wing. Wispy tendrils, chafing at their confinement had forced themselves loose and huddled gently by her hair-line, protective, daring a hand to come and move them, daring the observer to better admire their owner's high, finely structured cheek-bones. Her velvet-lashed lids framed eyes of stunning aquamarine —by far the most beautiful he'd ever seen. Just below her left outer eye was a dark mole, almost concealed by face powder.

It was her all right; he'd stake his life on that. He glanced down at the sheet of cabin allocations. A quick shuffle. There. A better cabin already.

'Let me take your bag, ma'am.'

Grateful to be rid of some of her burden, Adelaide handed him her heavy bag and moved towards the gangplank. Her last steps on English soil. Her first steps towards freedom.

Holding Daniel tightly to her bosom, she moved carefully along the gangway, straddling both worlds, belonging to neither.

As she took her final step off the gangplank onto the ship and a new life of freedom, Luke Collins took her elbow in a firm but gentle grip. A surge of warmth raced from her elbow up her arm, blossomed to the rest of her body. Adelaide felt safer and more secure than she had since her wedding day and raised her eyes to meet his. 'Thank you.'

Tanned and thickset, every inch of him appearing to be solid muscle, Luke Collins gazed back. His eyes were a deep winter grey, the color of a moorland storm. He smiled, easy, playful, with just a hint of arrogance, a smile so enchanting it would have drawn a cormorant from its fishing grounds.

Adelaide gave a shy smile in return and dropped her eyes to her baby. It wouldn't do to be noticed now. At all costs she must do nothing that would cause her to be recognized or removed from the ship.

'Follow me.'

On the quay crowds of people stood waving Union Jacks and shouting 'good-bye' to passengers. They skirted the deck, until finally they went indoors, and Luke Collins stopped in front of a staircase leading below decks.

'Let me take the baby for you. The steps are steep, until you get used to them.'

Are you in your right mind? she thought. She didn't know this man. Had he ever held an infant before? How could she trust him? How did she know he wouldn't run off with Daniel? But Luke Collins was a sailor. For reasons she couldn't identify she felt absolutely safe with him. So she handed over her infant son, her most precious treasure. To a total stranger.

Skillfully, he took the baby and cradled it against his powerful chest, as if he'd been born to perform that very act. When his back was turned to Adelaide his strong fingers deftly pushed back the blankets around the baby's face before swiftly rearranging them, and when she had negotiated the stairs, he returned the warm bundle to her and continued down the long corridor with Adelaide following.

At the far end of the passageway he stopped in front of a cabin door, pulled a set of keys from his pocket, selected one and thrust it into the lock. The door swung open effortlessly.

'Your cabin, ma'am.'

Adelaide was about to enter when she stopped. 'I can't go in there.'

'It's the best we have ma'am.'

'I'm quite sure it is.' Adelaide stepped inside and looked around. 'It just isn't for me.'

She watched as he strode through the sitting room, past the two lavishly upholstered arm-chairs, the mahogany writing desk, and bookcase filled with books, and opened a door on the far side.

'This is the bedroom, and the bathroom is just off it. I'm sure you'll find it quite comfortable once you get used to it.' He coughed. 'It doesn't usually take too much getting used to, ma'am.'

Adelaide felt flustered. This was just the environment she was escaping from. 'I'm sure it doesn't. It's just...I'd booked a budget cabin and...'

Her chest grew tight. This cabin had the stamp of James Rawtenstall all over it. Calm down, she told herself, don't make a scene, you'll arouse suspicion. She cleared her throat and met his gaze. 'There must be some mistake.'

'No mistake Mrs. ... Aspinall. This is the cabin that's been assigned to you. Unless of course, you wish to take up the matter with the purser. Or even the Captain.'

'Of course not,' said Adelaide, not wishing to draw further attention to herself. 'It's just...I'd feel more comfortable in a budget cabin.'

'The budget cabins are all taken,' replied Luke with care. 'You were upgraded because you're traveling alone with an infant. What's so wrong with that?' he asked, his tone bland, his words utter masculine reason.

'Nothing.' replied Adelaide flatly. 'Thank you.'

How could she possibly tell him it reminded her of all she was running from? The comfortable surroundings that hid dreadful secrets. The Rawtenstall household that told of betrayal and menace beyond belief.

There was a knock on the door. 'Mrs. Aspinall's cabin trunk's here, sir,' said the cabin boy.

'Thank you. I'm sure Mrs. Aspinall would like it in her bedroom.' Winter grey eyes locked with aquamarine ones. 'Wouldn't you?'

A warmth flushed up Adelaide's neck. 'Thank you,' she replied as the cabin boy left.

'I'll leave you to unpack. We sail in two hours time.'

Luke walked through the door and closed it softly behind him, leaving a sense of something missing in his wake.

Left alone, Adelaide felt disquieted. If James Rawtenstall knew she was leaving, he'd already have had her dragged from the ship. He wouldn't arrange a luxury cabin for her, would he? So why did she feel trapped? Luke Collins seemed sincere enough. She'd felt so safe when he guided her along the deck by the arm. He'd held Daniel as if the little baby were made of porcelain. Her instincts told her he was a good man. So why was she uneasy? Just nerves, she reassured herself and looked around to inspect her premises. The gentle rays of the morning sun fell upon a large wooden bedstead.

A gentle knock on the door drew Adelaide out of her reverie. The door opened and a cabin boy stood in the frameway, holding a baby cot, already made up with sheets and blankets.

She smiled and motioned for it to be placed beside her bed. As soon as it was in place the cabin boy left.

Adelaide drew back the blankets and placed her sleeping infant in his cot. In three weeks time she'd meet her new husband-by-proxy. A man she'd never met, never even corresponded with. Still, it was a small price to pay for her escape from James Rawtenstall. At least she would be able to bring up her son in safety, far away from his influence.

She reached into her bag and drew out a key, inserted it into the lock of the cabin trunk, slid the catches aside and began to unpack their belongings. Daniel's first —she put his clothes in the two bottom drawers of the tallboy. She'd tried to bring enough clothes to last him until he was five years old. She wondered now if she'd brought enough. Knitting needles and wools she put in the third and fourth drawers up. Wool could always be reused, and she felt sure she would have enough.

Then her own clothes —not as many as she'd brought for Daniel, but then her needs would be fewer. Just a couple of 'good' dresses, several skirts and jumpers and some silk underwear. Her dresses and skirts she hung in the cabin wardrobe. The rest went into drawers.

Then came her embroidery silks and linens. And finally her treasures. So few of them really. But what she had she valued. There was a family portrait in a silver frame —her parents, brothers and sisters. It had been lovely belonging to a large family. The house had always seemed vibrant and alive, with people coming and going and friends calling. They hadn't had the money or the luxury of the Rawtenstalls, but they hadn't the 'deadness' of two people alone in a big house, with only one child to dote on. Now her family was all dead, but in her heart they were very much alive. They always would be. She placed the photo frame on the top of the tallboy and took out another photo in a matching frame. A photo of herself and Danny on their wedding day. She dusted a handkerchief over the frame, wiping away imaginary finger marks. Oh Danny, she thought, clutching it to her chest, what would you make of this mess?

She gazed deep into the photo, as if she could will him back to life. Danny's happy, honest face shone back at her, his eyes brimming over with boyish love. A love that they had both thought would last forever. As it had, in a way. Her eyes misted over, blurring the photograph. Danny was gone now, but she still had Daniel, Danny's final, lifelong gift to her.

She blinked, clearing her eyes, gazing again into the portrait. The radiant bride, standing beside Danny, laughing up into his eyes, seemed no more than a child. That's what they'd been really, young people, happy and optimistic, with a youthful love full of dreams and ideals that they'd thought would be everlasting. They'd had goals and plans that neither of them ever imagined would be unattainable. And Danny, thinking himself twelve feet tall and bulletproof, had gone off to war, to defend his wife, unborn child and country and had never returned.

Danny, the young man, would be saddened and angry at her

predicament. Whether he would have done anything about it she could only guess. But she knew without any doubt that he would want her to be happy and care for their child in the best way she knew how.

The girl in the picture, smiling at her husband with such pride and trust was long gone. In her place was a woman, frightened and alone, but determined to protect her baby at all costs. Somehow she sensed the young bridegroom would approve.

She trailed a finger across the glass, over the bridegroom's hair, across his eyes, down his cheeks, his lips, lingering there awhile. A tear slid unchecked down her cheek as she touched the photo to her lips in a final kiss good-bye. But the glass remained cold to her caress, the spirit of her dead husband having long departed. Carefully she wrapped the silver-framed photo in her bridal veil and placed it face down in her top drawer.

*****

Outside the cabin, the ship's hooter shrieked, sharp and high pitched. Adelaide jumped at the unexpectedness of it. From the bowels of the ship rose a low rumble. Dreadful though it sounded, she surmised it must be the drawing up of the anchors. Whistles blew, and Adelaide quickly crossed the cabin to the porthole and looked out. Slowly, the great ship was moving away from the quayside. The crowds waved, and some had even brought flags. Still she couldn't relax. Not yet. Not until they were far away from the shores of England.

Daniel was sleeping soundly, unaware of the potential danger around him. Adelaide touched her palm lightly to the downy hair covering his head. A surge of weariness washed over her as she walked into the lounge and slid bonelessly into a deep armchair, blanketing her face with her hands. For the first time since Danny had died she wept. A low, deep wail that washed up from the floor of her soul, dredging up with it all the tiniest remaining morsels of loss, the last fragments of anger.

She wasn't sure how long she sat alone, grieving for her

husband, her family and her life. When it seemed to her that she had no more tears left, she went into the bathroom, washed her face, brushed her hair till it shone and carefully applied a touch of lipstick.

'Today,' she told her reflection, 'is the first day of the rest of your life. Make it a good one.' She pulled her hair back from her face and was arranging it into a neat chignon when there was a gentle knock on her cabin door. She walked into the living area, crossed the floor to the door and opened it. A powerful Nordic invader, Luke's frame filled the doorway.

'We've upped anchor, and we're leaving. I didn't see you on deck. Is everything all right?'

She struggled for words. 'Er..yes, Officer Collins. Thank you.'

'Don't you want to wave to your friends and family?'

Adelaide hesitated. 'I've already said my goodbyes.'

'Is this your first sailing?'

Adelaide sensed the kindness in his words. It had been a long time since anyone had spoken to her with such consideration.

'Yes.' Heaven help her, this man was scrambling the words inside her head.

'In that case you might like to come up on deck. Come and see the able seamen decorating the ship. I'm sure you'll enjoy it.' He smiled with all the warmth of a sudden summer's day. 'Most people do.'

Adelaide hesitated, glancing through the bedroom door at Daniel still soundly asleep in his cot. Only another half hour and he'd need nursing again. She wanted to go, but she shouldn't. She'd promised herself to stay below decks most of the time. But this couldn't hurt, could it?

'All right. But only for a few moments.'

'Your baby will be quite all right here.'

'You've got experience, I suppose?'

'I'm not married, but I do like children.' He added, 'May I have just another peek at him before we go on deck?'

'Of course.' Always proud to show off her son, Adelaide led the way into the sleeping quarters. She'd had little enough opportunity at home, and this interest in her proudest achievement made her realize how lonely and isolated she'd felt since Danny's death.

As they closed the cabin door and walked towards the stairs, Luke turned to her. 'On long trips like this we usually all end up on first name terms. Why don't you call me Luke? May I call you Margaret?'

Adelaide hesitated, almost giving away her proper name. She would have to be careful.

'By all means.'

'Margaret it is.' Luke's voice was rich and warm. 'A beautiful name, feminine and wise. I think it suits you.'

'Thank you.' Adelaide looked down at the carpet to hide the pleasure at hearing his compliment, and so she missed the slight smile of satisfaction that crossed his features.

* * * * *

With Luke at her side Adelaide stepped out onto the deck and into the sunshine. Large triangular streamers, red, white and blue, were strung high above the decks, the canvas flapping and rumbling in the wind, lending a carnival atmosphere and sending a thrill of anticipation through her body. The able seamen were indeed decorating the ship, but not in the way she had imagined. It seemed as if the entire crew, dressed in stunning white uniforms was standing on the bottom deck, facing the shore. Dark banded hats on every head, feet slightly apart and arms raised, they saluted England, a salute of recognition and farewell, as the great ship picked up speed, and the crowd on the quayside grew smaller and smaller till they seemed like ants feasting on a dinner plate.

Around them other passengers were exchanging pleasantries with each other and a wave of loneliness swept over her. Men and women, happy and laughing, young people joking, new friendships being formed. She wouldn't be able to join in things like that on this trip. Not if she was to keep her head down and avoid being noticed.

As the sailors stood at ease and broke ranks, Adelaide watched a young woman with shining platinum blonde hair, also clad in white, delicately raise her skirt to reveal a white garter on her thigh. The woman laughed as one by one the sailors took turns to kiss it.

'Is she a sailor's wife?' she asked Luke.

'No. She's one of the mail order brides. She's obviously intending to enjoy herself before she reaches Damnation Island.'

'She seems like quite a character.'

'Maybe.' Luke was noncommittal. 'A few days at sea will test her mettle.'

'Maybe Augustus Island will test it more.'

Again the playful, slightly arrogant smile eased into Luke's granite features. 'It'll do that all right.'

'Why do seamen call it Damnation Island?'

'Because it's stunningly beautiful. It rises without warning from the ocean. And it's surrounded by rocks and seaweed which make it an almost lethal landing place. Few people go there. Fewer still leave.'

It was then that the enormity of what she was doing hit Adelaide like a draught of cold air.

'What are the inhabitants like?'

'They're an unknown quantity.'

Adelaide's vision swam as her eyes filled with unshed tears.

Luke's rich voice cut through the haze in her mind. 'Farewells are always a bit emotional, even for us sailors. You'll soon feel better.'

Adelaide bent her head. She didn't want to meet his gaze, didn't want to become any more vulnerable than she already was. 'I've got to go and nurse my baby.'

'I'll take you to your cabin.'

'There's no need.' she replied, more curtly than she'd intended.

'There's plenty of need,' he corrected her. 'You're upset. Until you become used to the ship, all the corridors will look the same. We can't have your baby crying, because his mother's lost, can we?'

* * * * *

Luke left the beauty at her cabin door. So this was the woman he was charged with looking after. Adelaide Rawtenstall. He'd been warned she may travel in disguise and under an assumed name, and that warning had borne fruit. How glibly she'd lied about her name. And no doubt about other things. He recalled holding the baby in his arms, noting the small black mole beneath its left eye, identical to the mother's. This was Adelaide Rawtenstall and her child; he had no doubt of that.

He strode down the corridor towards the deck.

He loved the life at sea. Three square meals a day, plenty of exercise, the challenge of the elements and the meeting of new faces. The money was good, and a large portion of his salary he sent home to his mother for her to put aside for his sisters' education. Life had been hard for the Collins family since his father died, and Luke's financial contribution made all the difference to them. It also left enough money for him to enjoy himself when his ship stopped at various ports of call. His needs were few, and he was content with what he had.

Content that was, until James Rawtenstall had summoned him to his office and asked him to undertake this latest project. He'd never met the wealthy mill-owner until two days before the sailing. Rawtenstall had outlined the history of his son's brief marriage, sketched details of his death and stated his own wish to have his daughter-in-law and her son, for private reasons, returned by whatever means to England, where they could be well cared for. For this job alone, Luke would earn the equivalent of two years' salary at sea. There had also been the unspoken threat that if Luke didn't take the job, his family may well find themselves evicted from their rented cottage. Veiled but there nevertheless. Despite a nagging sense of unease, Luke had taken the job. It was nothing he could quite put his finger on, but he knew Rawtenstall had a reputation as a very mean man. Nevertheless, the man had paid fifty per cent up front, and Luke had accepted it. 'Good faith money' was how Rawtenstall had termed it.

As Luke mounted the steps to the noisy deck to carry out the rest of his duties, he recalled his father's last words to him as he lay dying. 'Do what's right and you won't come to any harm.'

He didn't know the right and wrong of this yet, but he'd make sure his family was all right. He'd return Adelaide Rawtenstall to her father-in-law, as he had been paid to do. As an honorable man, he wasn't happy with it. But it could turn out that Adelaide Rawtenstall was a bad woman, doing the Rawtenstall heir a very bad turn. Or she could get cold feet, and his job of returning her would be easier. He'd have to wait and see how things panned out. Time had a great way of showing the correct direction to take. In the meantime he'd keep his observational senses wide open and do the best he could. One way or another.

He pulled at the front of his jacket, straightened his sleeves, organizing the outer man as well as the inner man and walked briskly, officer-style, arms by his sides, to the deck. As he went about his duties he began formulating a plan.

* * * * *

An hour later, Luke Collins had completed his work. All the passengers were comfortably in their cabins. Dinner was being prepared in the large kitchens, the sailors had checked the lifeboats and lifebelts, the ship was as seaworthy as it always was, and both passengers and crew were aware of evacuation procedures, should the need arise. He knew what he had to do, but it didn't rest easy with him. Adelaide Rawtenstall's demeanor disturbed him. When he'd taken her on deck her eyes had held a wariness beyond her years. That wariness could well be in keeping with her current actions. But they had been red-rimmed. She'd been weeping. Why exactly? Her cabin had been neat, with a silver framed portrait on her chest of drawers. There was a distinct resemblance among all of them. Obviously a family photo, taken several years ago by the looks of things. She looked different now. More haunted than tired or down-trodden. But that could well be due to the death of her husband, however caused.

Then there had been the trickle of unease that had inched down his spine when he recalled her reaction to his dismissal of the inhabitants of Damnation Island.

There was something about her he couldn't quite put his finger on. Something that didn't quite ring true with the information he'd been given about her. More, she possessed a special beauty, he suspected inner as well as outer. Her eyes, as clear as moorland pools, held all the warmth and promise of an eastern night —and hid more than a sprinkling of wariness. There was something else, too, something about her rapid and occasionally jerky movements that suggested...fear? But of what? Could it be she had good reason to flee Rawtenstall? If she did, he could only guess at the treatment she'd receive when he returned her.

Luke Collins liked this situation less and less. He'd let Rawtenstall know Adelaide was sailing, but he'd also do some investigating of his own. Something didn't quite add up. He was determined to discover exactly what.

He strode into the radio room, seated himself and began to radio a message ashore.

CHAPTER TWO

The three-storey house, its grey stones hewn from granite, kept its eternal vigil on the edge of the wind-swept moor. Around the eaves the wind shrieked and howled so loudly that the man inside almost missed hearing the thump-thump-thump of the knocker on the stout oaken door.

The parlour-maid was finished for the day. His wife was busy. With a snort of disgust James Rawtenstall strode impatiently down the hallway, through the vestibule and pulled open the front door. In the lamplight, hair haloed by frost and moonlight, stood a delivery boy. 'Waken the dead, would yer?'

'Mr. Rawtenstall?'

'Who the hell else would answer my door?'

'Telegram, sir.'

James Rawtenstall snatched the envelope from the boy's hand.

'Will that be all, sir?'

'Course it's all. Yer don't expect a bloody tip, do you?'

The boy shook his head.

'Be on yer way, then. Afore I set the dogs on yer.'

'Yes sir. Very good sir.'

Rawtenstall kicked his door shut, strode back down the hallway tearing open the envelope and reading the contents as he went.

'Confirm Adelaide Rawtenstall and baby on board SS *Neptune.* Will contact later.'

James Rawtenstall balled the telegram and threw it onto the parlor fire.

Blast the whore's eyes!

He'd suspected the scum-bag might do something like this. He'd known she'd made enquiries, of course. No member of his family could move far without his being aware of it. But in his heart he hadn't really believed she'd go through with her scheme.

She needed to be reminded of just who was the boss in his family. Not that she was part of it. She was merely the hatching-house for his beloved grandson and could now be discarded. He would have done so immediately after the birth, if he'd been in his right mind.

When he got his hands around her throat, he'd show her so firmly who was boss, she'd beg his permission to breathe in and thank him for his permission before she breathed out again.

Collins was going to earn his money! And if he had to persuade Collins to do anything illegal, Collins would have to look to his own neck, and James Rawtenstall would be in the clear. That was life, and life was tough. The tough life had taken his son, his Danny. Danny hadn't needed to go to war. He could have stayed at home as a key worker, been excused military duties. But no, he wouldn't listen to his father who had his best interests at heart. He'd had to prove himself to that slip of a wife of his. Not that he should have had anything to prove to a slut from the rental cottages. But the boy wouldn't see sense, so under the thumb he was. He'd gone and enlisted, and this was the result. A grandson could have filled the gap. James Rawtenstall, mill-owner and property holder, could have brought the lad up just like Danny. Taught him how to be a man. Could have taken him fishing, hiking. Built trolleys for him to race with his friends. He could have carried on the Rawtenstall line. And now he, too, was gone.

Striding out of the parlor he ignored his wife, who was knitting as usual. Always doing something with her hands, never anything with her mind, like all women. He slammed into the kitchen, snatched his greatcoat from its hook, thrust his arms through the sleeves, opened the back door and strode out into the night.

Striking out through the darkness, with the wind pulling his oiled hair flat against his scalp, his feet crossed the heather in a seemingly random direction. Damn Danny for going to war and causing this mess. Damn him. Damn him. And damn his own wife for her secondary barrenness in being unable to produce more children. But most of all, damn his daughter-in-law for stealing his son's affection and love and for whisking away his grandson after he'd offered to buy the child from her. He stumbled across the moorland, his arms windmilling furiously around his head, as if to ward off some unspeakable evil. He roared his terrible pain to the winds, and the winds bore it away with them, dispersing it to the far corners of the moor, where even the sturdy heathers bent as if unable to withstand the insupportable grief.

Eventually he came upon the Fallen Stones and, prostrating his sobbing form on them, fell finally into a deep slumber.

He awoke in the morning to find the last of winter's icy tentacles had wrapped themselves around his limbs and joints, rendering them cold and stiff. But his mind was as sharp and as crystal clear as it had always been. An eye for an eye, that's what the Bible said. Always a church-going man, that was the teaching he'd follow. To the letter. No-one, not even family, especially not family, crossed James Rawtenstall and got away with it.

He was going to get the baby back. The Lord in his wisdom would understand. After all, Danny and his wench had wanted a girl. He'd bring the lad back to where he rightfully belonged. He was a Rawtenstall. The lad was a Rawtenstall and heir to his grandfather's empire. He deserved only the best. And only his grandfather could provide it.

His mind now completely in order, confident in the knowledge of what he was going to do, James Rawtenstall stood up and headed in the direction of home.

CHAPTER THREE

Four days out to sea and the North Atlantic Ocean was calm. Occasionally a wisp of cloud, seeking, but not finding a storm, crossed the pale skies. Beneath the heavens the ocean was a deep sapphire blue, all-knowing, all-seeing, judging none who sailed upon her. The Lord was in his heaven, and all was right with the world.

On board SS *Neptune*, the gaily colored banners that had rustled so cheerfully in the wind as the ship left England were long gone. Adelaide couldn't say for sure when they'd been taken down as she had spent the last few days in her cabin.

She'd spent her time nursing Daniel, cuddling him and singing soft lullabies. At night, lulled by the gentle cat-lapping of the water against the hull of the ship, they'd both slept soundly, Daniel with the innocence and trust of a neonate, Adelaide enfolded by dreams of the loving warmth of her deceased family and inspired by memories of her fun-loving husband, waking only when sunlight streamed through the cabin porthole and a hot cooked breakfast was served by the cabin boy.

As a result, she felt refreshed and calm. So refreshed and calm that on the morning of the fourth day, she wrapped Daniel in a warm, blue crocheted shawl and ventured onto the deck with him to watch the waves and smell the sharp freshness of the maritime air.

As she stood on the deck, Adelaide tasted a slight sea-saltiness on her lips, brought there by a breeze as gentle as swansdown. The sun was thrusting its tawny head above the velvet horizon, and the deck was as empty and as quiet as the ghost of the *Marie Celeste.* Her footsteps whispered across the wooden deck as she crossed to the helm with her infant, enjoying the quiet, the stillness.

The breeze grew stronger, caressing her face as gently as a lover's kiss, and she watched the sun's crimson carpet roll out across the sky, painting the distant waters a rich vermillion. Around them, as far as the eye could see, the ocean lay mirror-smooth, like polished copper, the only audible sound the pulse of the engines and a gentle hiss as the ship ploughed a furrow through the immense body of water that was the open sea. No bird sang, no fish leapt from its feeding grounds.

So engrossed was Adelaide in the beauty, the gentleness of nature that special morning, she didn't hear the quiet pad of footsteps behind her.

Therefore his matter-of-fact words 'Enjoy it while you can,' took her completely by surprise.

Adelaide's heart stopped briefly, then began to hammer a rapid drumbeat in her chest as the blood left her head, rushing for the sanctuary of her feet.

She whirled around, and as Luke Collins' handsome face filled her field of vision, her back slid noiselessly down the metal rails, and she half-slumped onto the deck.

'Give me your baby and put your head between your knees.'

'No,' she countered, her voice far away in her own ears.

'Margaret, I'm here to protect you. And your baby.'

Gently but firmly he took Daniel and forced her head downwards, till the wave of giddiness receded.

When she was able to raise her head, he checked her pulse. A little fast, but otherwise she was fine. 'You're very lucky I was here.'

'Why's that?'

'Because you nearly fainted.'

Her gaze was unsteady, but accusing. 'You gave me the fright of my life!'

'By speaking to you?'

Recovering by the second, Adelaide retorted, 'Enjoy it while you can. What was that supposed to mean?'

'Merely that there's a storm brewing.' He watched her closely, his eyes narrowing into dark fathomless slits. 'What else could it mean?'

Adelaide stood up shakily, gripping the rail. 'Understand this, Luke Collins. If you ever think of scaring me like that again, I'll slap you senseless. It was a beautiful morning till you came along!'

Snatching Daniel from his arms she returned unsteadily below decks, promising herself never to lay herself open to surprises like that again. She was far too jumpy. It could only arouse suspicion if it happened again.

* * * * *

Back on the deck, Luke cursed his own stupidity. Everyone, even the hunted, deserved to enjoy a beautiful sunrise once in a while. Her reaction was not what it would be if she were the evil woman James Rawtenstall had painted her to be. If Rawtenstall were correct, surely she would be abandoning her baby for hours on end, behaving unbecomingly with the sailors and generally acting like some sort of hussy. No, he surmised, James Rawtenstall was wrong in this matter. And now he, Luke, had ruined the sunrise for her and for a part of himself, too.

He'd have to be careful she didn't suspect him. She was jumpy enough as it was.

True, he hadn't intended to scare her in quite the way he did. He'd wanted only to test a theory. It was now well and truly tested, and Luke was not proud of himself. Whatever Margaret Aspinall, or Adelaide Rawtenstall, to give her her real name, had or hadn't done, she was doing her best to get her life in order. Her cabin was immaculate. Her baby was well-clothed and well-nourished. She displayed photos of her family by her bedside. And she certainly wasn't flirting with every sailor available or unavailable, as were some of the other women. He had to wonder what on earth she'd ever done to incur James Rawtenstall's wrath. Rawtenstall was a bad man to get on the wrong side of, as his own family knew well.

This mission was becoming complicated. The more he saw of her, the more attracted to her he became, and that only made his task that much more difficult.

What he wanted to do was take her in his arms, plunge his fingers through her shiny raven hair, fall into the depths of her aquamarine eyes. He wanted to place his lips on hers, kiss away her fears, see her eyes ignite for him. He thrust away the seeds of those thoughts before they could germinate in his emotions. He needed complications in exactly the same way a school of fish needed a blackboard.

But he could make the rest of the day better for her and thus take the first step towards salving his conscience.

* * * * *

Back in her cabin, away from the social whirl of life on deck, Adelaide knelt by the baby-bath, washing Daniel in warm soapy water, delighting in touching his soft baby skin. She splashed him with water as he laughed up at her. He was almost enough to take her mind off Luke. Almost enough to make her forget the touch of Luke's strong hands, his deep caressing voice, even the way he'd held little Daniel in his arms.

If she wasn't so afraid of James Rawtenstall, she wouldn't have been so jumpy with Luke. The fact that she was a married woman, even if proxy-married, should have afforded her some notion of safety, comfort even.

James Rawtenstall hadn't had her dragged from the ship before it sailed from England, and the ship hadn't turned back. Now if he attempted to harm her or Daniel he would have her new husband to answer to.

Maybe.

But her new husband didn't know about Daniel, did he? What would his reaction be? If he didn't like children, she'd have to live somewhere else. She'd cross that bridge when she came to it. For the moment, she had to get to Augustus Island safely. Four days into the voyage she had nothing to fear. Had she?

Hi Gill,

A little bird told me you were looking for some light holiday reading so look what the Xmas fairy has brought!

Enjoy!

Liz

When Adelaide had finished bathing and nursing Daniel she carried him into their bedroom, put him down to sleep and sat down to embroider a table-cloth for her new home, her fingers pushing the needle with its colored threads trailing through the linen to form a picture of snow-covered Pendle Hill. This was the view from the bedroom she'd shared with her sister as a child. She loved the view, loved the sudden warmth in the air just before the first snows fell. Slowly, the concentration required for the structured work eased the rawness of her fear, so when the knock came, she calmly put her embroidery aside and opened the cabin door.

Clad in jeans and a tee-shirt, tanned, muscled and holding a large fish, mouth still attached to the hook, stood Luke, smiling comfortably. If he'd been offended by her earlier threat to slap him senseless he showed no sign of it.

'In the Middle East, showing an animal's eyes is a way of showing how fresh the meat is. Besides,' he added with a wry smile, 'there isn't a flower-seller on board.' He held the fish up high for her to inspect. 'Will you accept this gift to let it be cooked, as a token of how truly sorry I am for upsetting you this morning?' When Adelaide didn't speak, he added, 'I caught it for you myself.' He hesitated a moment. 'Naturally, if you don't want it....'

'Of course,' she said, wanting to make amends herself. She hesitated slightly, not wanting to draw further attention to herself, but not wishing to appear churlish either. Then the words spoke themselves. 'But only if you'll promise to eat it with me.'

'Very well, Madam.' He bowed long and low. 'I'll give orders to the cook.'

Adult company would be good for her, she thought, pushing away momentarily her promise to remain sequestered alone in her cabin for the rest of the voyage.

'You may arise now, Sir Luke.' Adelaide touched his shoulder and blushed. Luke blushed too, as he began to rise.

* * * * *

Much later, inside Adelaide's living area, the lamps were

dimmed in their sconces. From the music box at the corner of the writing desk, a soft melody drifted through the room. 'That was beautiful Luke. Thank you,' Adelaide said as the cabin boy removed the remainder of the fish and vegetables they'd eaten for lunch.

'There's one more thing I have to do to make up for this morning.'

'You've more than made up for it, Luke. Besides if I hadn't been so jumpy about...' She stopped herself just in time. '...about being alone it wouldn't have happened.' Adelaide shot a sideways glance at Luke. He didn't appear to have picked up on her hesitation. But if things were different ...

'Margaret,' He took her small hand gently in his big one, stroked his finger tips along her nails and lifting it to his lips, gently kissed the tips of her fingers. 'I spoiled the sunrise for you this morning. There's a wonderful view I'd love to show you. Few passengers have the opportunity to see it. Fewer still are brave enough to give it a try.'

'I'm brave enough,' she replied levelly. 'I don't scare easily.' Careful, she thought, make sure your words are compatible with your actions. You've still got a lot to lose. James Rawtenstall could yet find you.

Of course you're brave enough, he thought, otherwise you wouldn't even be on this trip. He said, 'That's it then. You'll come?'

'Where to?'

'Remember I told you a storm was coming?'

'I'm not likely to forget, am I?'

'I'd like you to see both the placid beauty that surrounds us and the upcoming storm. The storm won't hit till much later. But I'd like to take you to a ...high vantage point.'

'How high?'

'The crow's nest.'

'You're joking!'

'You'll come to no harm. I'll be with you every step of the way. I haven't lost a passenger yet.'

'How many others have you taken up?'

'None. But I've shown plenty of seamen.'

'Daniel should sleep for an hour or so. Can you find a baby-sitter?

'Yes. Just for an hour or so. That will be time enough.'

Enough to show you the crow's nest, he thought. Not enough for what I'd like to share with you. Not enough for me to pull down the wall you've built around yourself. I'd do it slowly, lovingly, so you'd learn to trust me. Brick by brick. You'd trust me so much the final bricks would crumble down, and you'd never mortar them together again.

'Dress warmly. There will be a breeze up there.'

* * * * *

Ten minutes later, wearing trousers, sweater and flat shoes, her hair pulled back into a neat chignon at the back of her head, Adelaide ascended the rat-lines. Luke was behind her, his hands following her hands, his feet following her feet, lest she should slip and fall.

The freshening wind blew a strand of hair across her eyes, reducing her vision. She lowered her head to shake it away and froze. Below her on the deck, sailors like miniature characters who would have fitted into a doll's house, moved about their work, while around them passengers took constitutionals around the ship. All that was between her and the people below on the deck were the strands of rope she was climbing. If she missed her footing she would crash to the deck to land at their feet in a tangled mess of broken bones and splattered blood.

'Just keep going,' Luke urged behind her, his breath warm on her neck, their bodies almost but not quite touching. 'You won't fall. But if you do, I'm here to catch you.'

She couldn't help but feel Luke had always been there. From the minute she first set her foot on board ship. And she hadn't come to any harm. It seemed like he'd been there for a life-time.

Adelaide raised her right hand and grasped the next hold. Then her right leg. Then her left hand, her left leg, and before she realized it, she was ascending rapidly again.

'I'm all right. I just thought I'd have a look at the view,' she lied.

'Save it for the top. It's much better.' Luke's warm breath fanned her neck. 'Just keep going. You don't want to settle for second-best, do you?'

Again the warm caressing tone, the subtle hint of musk from his skin pervading her senses, rendering her even more aware of his every move. If she leaned back just a fraction she would be in his arms, in full public view, suspended from the rat-lines for all to see.

Adelaide sighed. 'I've had my chance at first best. I won't get that again. Second best will have to do.'

Did she imagine she could feel his taut masculine length covering her body, protecting her, caressing her?

'I'm with you, Margaret. You need fear nothing.'

How right he was. For this moment of time they shared the world. And at the end of the trip was her new husband, a man she hoped to be able to grow to love. If she allowed Luke into her emotions it would only make her proxy marriage more difficult. Suddenly it was too much, the loss of Danny, the threats from her father-in-law, her stranger husband. And meeting Luke.

A gentle breeze stirred Adelaide's hair. If she had Luke in her life, by her side, she would fear nothing. Together they could hack a niche for themselves in the rock-face of life. Start a dynasty where they and their children would be fearless, grasping life by both hands, harnessing it, answering to no-one. She shook herself. What on earth had she been dreaming of? It was just that Luke felt so...right. She allowed herself a moment's freedom, glorying in the exhilaration of the day, thrilling when the wind whipped across her face, dreaming of what might have been. It was at this moment that Adelaide knew, without any shadow of doubt, that she'd mortgaged her soul and her youth for the precarious safety of a proxy marriage with a stranger she'd never met.

With this realization, the ascent of the rat-lines seemed more difficult than before. But with it also came the confidence of knowing that if she allowed it, she could love again. Thus, inch by painful inch, her fear dissipated, and she gained a new sense of power in her abilities.

After what seemed an endless and trying journey for both body and mind, she reached the top. Only the hurdle of climbing into the arched crow's nest remained, and she would be there.

'Close your eyes,' said Luke behind her. 'There's nothing to be afraid of. There's just you and me.'

'I can't go any further, ' Adelaide gasped.

'Of course you can. Hold onto the platform. I'll do the rest.'

Adelaide closed her eyes as her hands grasped the hard wooded edge. She felt Luke's strong arms encircle her waist, lift her gently, tenderly, higher and higher. She felt the wooden platform nudge her thighs, Luke's tender hands on the flare of her hips, and when she opened her eyes, she was standing on the top of the world —with Luke beside her. Together they gazed out over their new horizon. The sight took her breath away. All around them, the entire three hundred and sixty degrees, the oceans and sky met as if they and Luke and Adelaide were guests awaiting the start of an outrageous party.

The breeze that on deck had been a caress was now a fierce wind, pulling and tugging at her hair, loosening it from its chignon, threatening to tumble it around her shoulders.

Gently Luke placed a great palm on her shoulder.

'Don't move an inch,' he breathed.

She didn't.

Tenderly, his touch no more than a whisper of thistledown, he unpinned the rest of her hair, and it cascaded about her shoulders to ripple between them, an obsidian current, wild and untamed.

Winding its length around his hands, he lifted it to his face, pressing it to his strong Nordic cheeks before raising it high across her field of vision, blanketing her from the world, its beauty and its badness. Then he allowed it to cascade from his fingers like a dark waterfall tumbling into a pool of magic blackness. She felt feminine and powerful.

No man had ever made her feel like this before. Not even her husband, before his untimely death.

With a sense of despair Adelaide knew she wanted Luke. But she was married by proxy to a man with whom she hoped to carve out a meaningful life. A man she hoped would provide safety for herself and her baby, at least until Daniel was a man.

She wanted Luke as she'd never wanted Danny and realized her proxy marriage was just another prison sentence. For eighteen years she wouldn't be able to consider any man other than her husband. Danny had sacrificed himself, for her, Daniel and England. But it had been quick. Her sacrifice would be at least eighteen years. Maybe a lifetime. Putting herself and her own needs and wants aside for little Daniel. Life shouldn't be like this.

'You have the most beautiful hair. This is how you should wear it. As free as the winds, as wild and untamed as the depths of the ocean. It lights up your eyes, your soul.' His hand brushed her shoulder. 'Shows you for the beautiful woman you are. Not that it's my business.'

Adelaide wanted to cry, to shout, 'It should be your business, Luke. We should have had a chance together.' But she didn't.

Instead she said, 'Tell me about the weather at sea, Luke.' Or anything else to keep my mind away from you. You're forbidden to me.

* * * * *

Luke wanted to place his lips upon hers, taste them with his. He wanted to explore the sweet recesses of her mouth. He needed to feel the feminine softness of her skin against his. But he had a job to do. Two, he amended silently. He had promised to return her and the baby to England, to James Rawtenstall. He also needed to find out for himself her side of things. An emotional involvement might well take care of that but not in the long term. It would only complicate matters and probably add to her ultimate burden.

Luke's face cleared, all emotion clawed from it, and relaxed into a smile that would have parted the waters, had he been facing in that direction. When he spoke, his voice was like welcome dew upon velvet moss, caressing her ears, her eyes, her spirit.

'The weather at sea is like a woman. Beautiful one minute, savage the next —sometimes both at the same time. Inspiringly tempestuous, heart-warmingly calm. Spirited and fickle. You never know for sure where you are with her. Ignore her warning signs and she'll break you!'

Adelaide wanted to reach out a hand, touch the roughness of his cheek, the corded muscles of his neck, touch the springy chest hair outlined beneath his tee shirt, wrap her arms around the jeans that hugged his taut hips, molding his maleness.

She dragged her eyes away from him. 'What a poet you are. Do you see all of life like this?'

'Only the special aspects,' he said, his voice harsh, an edge of raggedness to it. 'Tell me something about yourself.' His hand lifted the curtain of hair from her cheek, stroking it behind one ear. 'I want to see your eyes light up when you tell me what makes your heart sing.'

He was so close she could hear his heartbeat, almost feel the blood pulsing through his veins. She lowered her eyes lest he should be able to read her thoughts. She wanted to tell about the hopes and dreams she'd shared with Danny, hopes she now held for herself and her baby. The dreams she would like to have shared with him, maybe, had things been different. But that would be disloyal to...whom exactly? She didn't know her proxy husband. Here on top of the world there were only the two of them. Who could she possibly be disloyal to?

Luke controlled his rapid breathing and, studying her carefully, saw the shadows cross her face and pressed further. 'Your son is the joy of your life.' It wasn't a question.

Adelaide nodded.

'Shall we start with him?'

'No.'

'His father?'

Luke watched the flush rise up Adelaide's neck and cheeks, saw the tears well in her eyes, pool there unshed. His long appraising look took in her hesitation. These were the emotions of a grieving and passionate woman, not the maladjusted waif James Rawtenstall had described.

What he wanted to do was take her in his arms, kiss the hurt and fear from her eyes. He wanted to tell her she'd never have to worry about anything ever again. He could provide a safe haven for her and her baby, care for them, provide for them. He wanted to warm her bed at night. But first he had to get her to admit, by some means or other, that she was Adelaide Rawtenstall, not Margaret Aspinall.

'Danny... ' She stopped, fighting back the words and the tears.

"I'm sorry.' He paused, then went on. 'Tell me about your home.'

'I come from the edge of the moors, Luke.' Her voice was still shaky.

'Isn't that an inhospitable place to live?'

'Not really. It's a wild place where the summer breezes bend the heathers, and mists come quickly and heavily.' She ventured a smile at the memory. 'In winter the winds blow cold and harsh forcing the snow to swirl between cracks in the doors.' Her tone lightened. 'We build peat fires indoors and bake bread and scones.' A smile of dazzling brilliance crossed her features, bringing a joyful curve to her lips, a light to her eyes. 'And when twilight draws close, the wind streams through the moorland stones. And in the mornings after the snow, a thick silence lies all around.'

She gazed beyond him into the distance, a happy, faraway look in her eyes.

'You loved it there, didn't you?'

'Very much. Some mornings I wake up on ship and imagine I can smell the peat fire, hear the wind. Then I open my eyes and find it was just a dream.'

'It's not too late to go back, Margaret.'

'For me it is.'

Luke trailed a finger down her cheek, below her jawline, tilting her chin upwards so her eyes met his.

'Did you love your husband?'

'Very much. But he's dead now, and I've got to do the best I can for Daniel.'

Tears flooded Adelaide's eyes. She shook her head and turned away. 'I can't tell you any more, Luke.'

Luke came up behind her, put his hands on her shoulders, 'You've got a lot of living to do, Margaret. There's a whole world waiting for you to explore with the right man. You should give that some serious thought before you disembark at Damnation. If you wish to return with the ship, I'll guarantee your free and safe passage home.'

The right man. Free and safe passage back to England. It was tempting. Very tempting. But no matter how tempting, Daniel's safety was paramount. If anything were to go wrong, she wouldn't get a second chance at Damnation Island. She had to stay on her original course.

'Look.' He turned her around, and the crow's nest swayed. Adelaide grabbed his muscled arm, heavily sprinkled with blond hairs. 'It's only a gust of wind,' he said, putting one arm firmly around her waist, pointing to the horizon with the other. Adelaide's eyes followed the direction he was pointing. In the far distance, scarcely visible to the naked eye, tiny flecks of white dotted the dark water. Wisps of cloud, like traces of candy floss traced the sky above them. On the edge of the horizon a thin streak of amethyst marked the ending of the ocean, the beginning of the heavens. A thread of light raced across the sky.

'That's the storm we'll sail into,' he said.

'Will it be dangerous?'

'Probably not. But it will be showy.'

'Have you ever been wrong?'

'Never.' But this time he might be. This storm could well be the mother of them all.

CHAPTER FOUR

In the dead of night the storm rushed in, buffeting the ship with savage ferocity, shrieking its anger around the cabin portholes. Through her restless dreams Adelaide stirred and pulled the warm bedcovers closer around her ears.

A flash of white lightning, vivid and forked, illuminated her cabin, waking the shadows in the corners. Then it flickered and died.

It was here, the storm Luke had predicted. Tender, strong and kind, he would probably be asleep in his own bunk. Reassured by this thought she counted the seconds. One...two...they seemed interminable as she waited for the distant rumble and growl of thunder. The eye of the storm was still some way off.

From the sitting room there was the sound of objects falling onto the floor.

Adelaide sat up in bed. She loved the metallic taste of the storm in her throat, the tangy smell of its fury in her nostrils and the stirring in her soul it caused. She loved storms; they gave her a sense of exhilaration, a feeling of power. If Damnation Island was as wild as she'd been told, she could settle there, make a home.

The ship rolled in the water as the first of the storm waves thundered into it. Wave after wave buffeted the great ship, lifting it almost vertical, dropping it into watery troughs, only to rise again and fall even lower than before. Did her new husband like storms? They'd have to take time to get to know each other, discover each other's inner workings. Explore each other's strengths, discover and understand each other's weaknesses. Just as she and Luke were doing. The thought brought her up with a jolt. She shouldn't be thinking of Luke in that way. He was forbidden to her, as she was to him. But she was confident she could make it work on Damnation Island. The knowledge that her family, had they been alive, would support her in this decision, as would Danny, was a great help.

Adelaide swung her feet out from the warmth of the bed to the cooler floor of the cabin, leaving thoughts and dreams of Luke indented in the soft pillow. In the sitting-room, she found the bookcase had disgorged its entire contents into an untidy heap. Adelaide straightened them and left them in tidy piles on the floor. There was little point in returning everything to its proper order until the storm had passed. Besides there was something more pressing, more urgent calling to her.

Daniel was sleeping soundly. As Adelaide tugged her sweater over her head and brushed her hair, she reassured herself that she was doing nothing wrong. She was only going out to watch the storm. To see how it compared to the ones that hovered for hours over the moors. She wasn't hoping to share it with Luke, was she?

She hurried down the corridor that led to the steps to the main deck. The lights were dim, casting eerie shadows in the darkened corners. When she reached the top of the steps she stood for a moment in the doorway, holding her breath. The blackness was total, and Adelaide could feel, rather than see, the giant breakers as they thundered across the deck, hear the water running in torrents from aft to stern, the gentle whooshing and clittering of bubbling sea-foam on the wooden boards as they left a trail of driftwood and seaweed in their wake.

She glanced skywards. The position usually occupied by the moon was vacant, no doubt usurped by the storm clouds. The great dark shapes shifted slightly, allowing a delicate shroud of light to pierce the sky. She used the light to crawl unsteadily across the wet deck and grasp the handrail, out of sight of the crew who were checking the lifeboats and life-rafts. She threw back her head to better feel the wind gallop across her face, through her hair, pulling it out behind her back like party streamers, before letting it bounce on her back like a rubber-ball on a string. The smell of ozone and salt spray was magnificent, exhilarating. She raised her face to the wildness of it. Beneath the ship, the ocean seethed in an angry cauldron of foam. Adelaide had never felt so vital, so alive. She laughed into the fury.

A ball of green lightning pulsed across the heavens, illuminating the entire night panorama, and fell across the waters near the ship. A grey wall of water rose from the ocean and washed the ship and Adelaide with it. She gulped, taking in air and salt water. The lightning flashed again, showing her a hunched shadow across the deck, kneeling by the rails.

Thunder exploded around the ship. Not the echoing rumble from the moorland storms; this was King Neptune and Mars, the God of War, locked in a death battle, and the ship was their battleground.

On the opposite side of the deck the figure rose and moved steadily six feet farther along the deck, to crouch again by the rails. How he managed to walk when she could barely stand she didn't know. More importantly, what on earth was he doing out on a night like this? Not storm-watching, that was for sure.

Busy watching the dark shape, she didn't hear the wave coming at her from behind. It hit her unexpectedly, wresting her grip from the rail and carrying her in its watery embrace across the deck. Her feet were lifted above the boards, her hands groping for purchase on something, anything, to stop her rapid voyage across the deck, before she went over the rails into the deep. Her head rose above the surface of the water, and as she gasped in air she slammed into something firm and muscled that took her into his arms.

There was no time to think, no time to fear, as the water receded. The shadowy figure clasped her in his strong arms, holding her tightly to a hard chest and carried her against him. She knew she no longer need fear. He was taking her to a place of safety, and that was all that mattered. Her and him. Her feet touched the wooden deck, and she was bent double over his arm, gagging the salt water from her lungs as he gently slapped the space between her shoulder blades.

The spasm over, she stood upright and, with chilled and

stiffened fingers, pushed her soaked and matted hair from her eyes to better see her rescuer. 'Thank —' she began.

'What the hell are you doing outside?' came the familiar voice, once soft and caressing, now harsh and biting in anger. 'Don't you know you could have got yourself killed?'

Luke!

'Is there a law against watching a storm?' she gasped.

'No law. Only common sense. What on earth possessed you to go on deck on a night like this? You could have been swept overboard.'

'But I wasn't, was I?'

'Through sheer luck. Are you suicidal or something?'

Adelaide pulled her saturated sweater away from her body, away from her nipples that had tautened in the wet and the cold. 'I'm neither suicidal nor anything else. Not that it matters.'

Her entire family was dead. Her father-in-law wanted to steal her child from her. The menace of his threats had forced her to flee her own country, seeking exile at the opposite end of the earth. She'd sold her body to a stranger in return for her own safety and that of her child. And the one man whom she sensed —knew —was her soul-mate, she couldn't have because she was proxy-married. She had a child to bring up. The long lonely years rolled ahead of her, like a red carpet laid out to welcome a reluctant bride.

Before Adelaide realized what was about to happen, Luke's arms snaked around her waist, drawing her close to him. His hand ploughed through her hair, drawing her head backwards. With a fierceness that stunned her, his lips fastened on hers, warm and firm. He kissed her with a depth and a passion she hadn't realized could exist. Her arm slid around his neck, her fingers buried in his thick hair as she drew him even closer.

Without warning he broke off the embrace, thrusting her away from him, his voice riven. 'Never ever let me hear you say that again.'

'Say what?'

'Not that it matters. You matter very, very much.' He took her hand in his strong warm grip and half-led, half-dragged her to her cabin and opened the door. 'Inside,' he said, 'into a hot shower. I'll be back in fifteen minutes to check on you.'

* * * * *

Needles of hot water stung her skin as they beat down from the showerhead. Luke had held her in his arms. It was better than she could ever have imagined. Finally she knew what it was like to be held in his embrace. She felt wonderful. It was far better than she could ever have anticipated. The kiss was brief, but hardly chaste! It was a lover's kiss, the kind of kiss that she had only ever dreamed about. The kind of kiss that made her feel like a woman. It was as well he'd broken it, because she doubted she'd have been able to.

As she rinsed the shampoo from her hair she acknowledged that her late husband, Danny, had been a boy. Luke was a man. They were universes apart.

Not for the first time she voiced to herself serious doubts about the wisdom of her proxy marriage. It had seemed like a good idea at the time, a way of ensuring Daniel's safety and her own. It had seemed like her ticket to freedom, an escape from the harsh realities of life in England. Now she was far from certain. Luke's offer to return her safely to England seemed better by the minute. Nevertheless, she'd made her choice and would have to stand by it. She wouldn't do anything to jeopardize Daniel's safety. He deserved the best she could do for him. She'd have to go carefully, make sure her heart didn't rule her head, lulling her into a false sense of security.

A barrier had been split tonight. She'd have to take care it wasn't cracked wide open.

* * * * *

Far below the South Atlantic Ocean, the tectonic plates shifted again. A bigger shift than before, sending a bubble of hot air into the vortex, causing a gentle ripple on the surface. In the middle of the ocean, the one small extra wave passed unremarked.

CHAPTER FIVE

Back home, moorland storms had always cleared the air, leaving Adelaide refreshed, her thoughts and emotions crystal clear, ready to face anything. She resolved that this storm would be no different.

As she stood in the dim light of her sitting-room, Adelaide wasn't cold; — the navy woolen skirt, white linen blouse and woolen cardigan to match her skirt were all she needed after the hot shower. She was toweling her hair dry when Luke, blond, tanned and windswept, opened the door and entered the cabin. In his hand he held a round brass tray bearing two crystal thimble-glasses filled with tawny liquid. He carried it to the occasional table standing at the right hand side of the writing bureau and carefully laid it down.

'I knocked, but you didn't hear with the noise from the storm,' he said, taking a glass and handing it to her. 'Drink this. It's a tot of rum to keep you warm.'

Again Luke was taking care of her. How wonderful it felt to have someone's protection after the many months of hard struggle.

'How's Daniel?'

She sensed rather than heard the hesitation in Luke's voice. 'Come and see.' Adelaide took Luke across the cabin, through the low doorway and into the bedroom. As they gazed at the sleeping infant snuggled beneath the warm blankets, he stirred and opened his eyes.

Gently Luke bent down and picked up the boy. The tiny scrap

of manhood looked up in surprise at the fully-grown man and smiled, kicking his legs and tiny feet with joy. 'You're going to be a football-player, aren't you?' The little boy smiled again and yawned. 'I think he's hungry, Mum.'

Luke ducked his head again as he returned through the doorway into the sitting room and when Adelaide sat down in an arm-chair, he settled Daniel into her arms and sat down opposite her.

'I'm off duty for a while. Do you mind if I stay while you feed Daniel?' When he saw her indecision, he added, 'I'm good at changing nappies!'

Adelaide hesitated. She shouldn't bare her breasts and feed Daniel in public. Such a thing just wasn't right, but Luke didn't feel like 'public'. He ...she reached for the word...belonged. As simple as that. She discreetly unfastened her blouse, taking care not to expose herself unduly to Luke.

And so they sat together, a contented trio in a warm room, very much at home with each other.

As Daniel latched onto Adelaide and began to suckle, Luke told her of his parents and his sisters, what a happy family they'd been until his father'd had an accident at the pit.

'Coal dust got in the miners' hair, eyes, ears and every wrinkle they had so they used to go to the public baths after work. But on Friday Dad always came straight home and put his pit helmet in the kitchen sink. One of the girls would wash it. Mum used to put the big tin bath in front of the fire and fill it with hot water. She'd wash his hair and scrub his back and when she shouted to us that he was out of the bath that was my signal to go to the chip shop. Fish and chips was our Friday night treat. Then we'd all play cards till bedtime. It was a very happy house. You'd like my Mum and my sisters, and I know they'd really take to you.'

That could never be, she knew. Adelaide sighed wistfully as she unlatched Daniel, put him over her shoulder, burped him, then nestled him on to the other breast.

'What happened?' she prompted gently, her voice soft.

'One Friday I was coming out of school. I was fourteen and

hoping to become a lawyer. The thrust and parry of courtroom politics seemed like fun. As we hit the school gates I could hear the wailing wee-wah of the sirens as the noise echoed off the hills. The sirens from the pit. The ones that only go off when there's a major emergency.' His face darkened. 'I knew straight away it was Dad. My gut just told me. I didn't go home; I went straight to the pit. Mum and my sisters were already there. All night we waited in the fog and the drizzle. It was miserable. All sorts of rumors were flying about. The truth was the shaft had collapsed, trapping thirty-two men. The rescue teams tunneled and by nine that night, thirty-one men were out; some were okay, some had minor injuries. Dad was the only one who hadn't been brought to the surface. People drifted away, leaving us and a few friends who brought soup and sandwiches. We waited until dawn. Finally Dad was brought out on a stretcher.' Luke sighed. 'He was wet, cold and broken. It took him three days to die. Mum lost the house that went with Dad's job and got a job at one of the mills, and I went to sea.' His face cleared. 'It was a good move. I send money home to help out and to pay for my sisters' education. That's almost finished. Then I can be my own man.'

'Do you still want to become a lawyer?'

'Yes, but only after I've seen the world and earned enough money to set myself up.'

Luke didn't mention James Rawtenstall or the fact that his mother and family were renting one of his houses. Nor did he mention the handsome payment he would receive for returning Adelaide to England. He didn't want to spoil things.

Daniel finished suckling, and Luke held out his arms to take him from Adelaide. She handed him over and, placing him expertly over his shoulder, Luke rubbed his back, carefully averting his eyes while Adelaide re-buttoned her blouse.

As the ship continued to dip and sway through the storm, Adelaide told Luke about her life with her family. She told him of her father, who taught languages at secondary school and of how he used to come home from school and read for an hour by the fire alone. It was his way of unwinding.

'After tea we all helped wash up. Then we'd sit by the big fire in the kitchen. Mum would read us stories —one for each child. Then she'd bath the little ones and put them to bed, and Dad would sing to them as they fell asleep. We all learned to tell stories. Every night of the week it was someone's turn at table, while the rest of us had pudding. I was seventeen and Danny was courting me when they all fell ill. I thought they had the flu, so I didn't call the doctor. I looked after them and thought they were getting better. But I was wrong, and by the time I called the doctor it was too late. They had diphtheria. We were isolated, of course, but all the nursing in the world couldn't help. They all died within a week of each other. I couldn't understand how I was spared. I still don't. I would have married Danny anyway, but with being upset, one thing led to another, and I fell pregnant with Daniel. The baby just speeded things up, that's all. Then Danny was killed at war, so I'm striking out for a new life.'

Adelaide deliberately didn't mention James Rawtenstall. Or the fact that he'd offered to buy her son. This was the first time she'd talked about her innermost grief. She'd dealt with that and was proud of it. She couldn't lean too heavily on Luke who, good man that he was, had his own ghosts to deal with. She had to be independent, capable and strong, emotionally as well as physically —for her son. And also for herself.

As he had promised Luke skillfully changed Daniel's nappy. They were closer now, Luke knew. He hadn't planned it this way. It had just happened. Like a family in every sense except the legal one. And the carnal one. That was what he wanted, but he hadn't realized it until just now. A beautiful wife. A good friend. Children. He'd provide for them all.

Adelaide relaxed in her chair. How natural this all seemed. She felt so at ease with Luke. And how easily he and Daniel had taken to each other. If Luke had wanted to share his life with her, as man and wife, would she have been able to refuse? She couldn't search for an answer. It was probably the effect of the storm on both of them, stimulating them into the exchange of confidences, the catalyst for this new intimacy. When it had passed she would revert to her original goal of being a good wife for her proxy husband and put all this behind her. Wouldn't she?

As they walked into her bedroom and laid Daniel to sleep, the great ship shuddered and moaned beneath their feet, and the question that had been nagging unspoken in Adelaide's mind surfaced.

'Luke, you were angry with me for being on deck in the storm. But what were YOU doing there?'

Luke raised an eyebrow and replied nonchalantly. 'Fishing.'

'You were...fishing?'

'Of course,' he replied, his eyes laughing. 'Most people will probably get seasick, but not all of them. Those who don't become sick will be frightened, think the entire journey a nightmare and not want to eat. So we get them through tomorrow's rough weather. Then we feed them fish. Psychologically that's the best thing for them.'

'I didn't see any fishing rods.'

'There weren't any. I dropped hand-lines from the rails. We've got enough fish for days to come.'

'Very clever,' laughed Adelaide.

''Just part of the service ma'am.' Luke rose from his chair, saluted her, drained his glass and glanced at his watch. 'I'm back on duty about now,' he said and strode from the cabin.

* * * * *

With Luke's departure the air in the cabin seemed colder, the shadows in the corners deeper and darker. Daniel was fast asleep. Adelaide crossed the cabin to the tallboy and from a lower drawer pulled out her embroidery. She took it into the sitting-room, sat down in the armchair vacated by Luke and started work. Yet the comforting rhythm of the needle as it breached the fine film of linen that had soothed her so well earlier no longer held the same healing magic. As the needle thrust through the material it tore the skin of her finger, drawing blood. Putting her finger to her mouth, she sucked the blood away and sipped the rum Luke had poured into her glass.

She tasted Luke. His lips on hers.

She was back on deck, his body pressed close to hers, his maleness taut against her belly. She wanted more of him. More of him running his hands through her hair, over her body. She wanted his touch. Shamelessly she wanted to touch him. No amount of embroidery would change that.

CHAPTER SIX

Even inside her own cabin Adelaide could hear the cries and moans of the sick passengers. She'd nursed her entire family through diphtheria and done it well, her only mistake being not realizing how sick they really were. She'd been a comfort to them, she knew that. Surely she could offer some assistance to the rest of the passengers now. Wasn't something better than nothing at all?

She checked Daniel. He was sleeping soundly.

She walked down the corridor of the lurching ship towards the sickbay. Chaos and panic had established a firm hold on all of the passengers and some of the crew. Rain peppered the portholes like bullets from a machine-gun.

The cream-colored walls of the corridor were lit by lightning, green and purple, followed mini-seconds later by a thunderclap so violent she thought her ear-drums would burst. As the ship rolled and swayed like a leviathan, the passengers groaned, with the fitter ones becoming green but managing to remain upright, and several of the less fit collapsing into convulsing mounds on the wet and slippery floors. Their moans of despair filled the air. No one could have imagined that only twenty-four hours previously they had been happy and laughing.

Adelaide assessed the situation as calmly as her pounding nerves would allow. She pushed open the doors to the sickbay and grabbed an armful of sick bags. Then she went back outside and began to distribute them to people who were well enough to use them.

Once they were all distributed, she collected back as many as she usefully could, and, willing herself not to feel nauseated, she backed through the swing doors into the sickbay, the used sick-bags in her hands ready for disposal. Inside the sickbay all the beds were occupied, and the floors were lined with mattresses serving as makeshift beds.

In a corner of the room a doctor in a white coat was busy suturing a large gash on a sailor's head. He stopped momentarily as he became aware of Adelaide's presence.

'You sick?' he inquired agreeably.

'I've come to see if I can help.'

'You're a nurse?'

'I'm not qualified, but I do have some experience.'

His smile was warm as his dark eyes met Adelaide's. 'The nurse here's sick. I'll take all the help I can get.' He finished suturing the man's wound. 'Would you bandage this patient's head, please?'

As she wound the bandage around the man's head and fastened it with sticking plaster, the doctor set about returning someone else's dislocated shoulder to its rightful position.

Quietly and systematically they worked, till the doors swung open again and through them fell a young woman sobbing hysterically, her wet hair plastered to her head, giving her countenance an unattractive skull-like appearance. Behind her came Luke, his face grim. He helped her to her feet, and she clung to his arm like a limpet stuck to a rock.

'Don't leave me,' she sobbed. 'You said we'd be all right. Stay with me, please.' A fresh paroxysm of sobs seized her.

'We're busy,' Luke said curtly. Across the top of her head his gaze met Adelaide's. 'Do what you can for her, will you?'

Coolly Adelaide surveyed the wrecked young woman. She was frightened, certainly. But sick? She doubted it.

She watched as Luke tried to unpeel her from his arm. The harder he tried, the more she clung. Had she no self-respect, Adelaide wondered.

The ship lurched sickeningly, and the woman threw her arms

around Luke's neck.

Luke wasn't smiling.

He appeared embarrassed as Adelaide walked over to them and put her arms around the young woman's shoulders. As the woman relaxed her death-grip on Luke, Adelaide walked her to a straight-backed chair across the room. With a damp cloth she mopped her forehead and dabbed at her wrists.

Drawing up a chair in front of her, Adelaide handed her a small paper cup filled with water. 'I'm Adelaide Rawtenstall. What's your name?' Lord, she'd given her proper name. Too late now. The woman was probably too upset to remember it.

'Beatrice Robinson.'

'Very well, Beatrice. Have you hurt yourself?'

'No.'

'Are you sick?'

'No.'

'So why are you crying?'

'I'm so scared.' She hiccupped a sob. 'I thought a cruise was supposed to be smooth. I never expected anything like this.'

'Beatrice,' Adelaide said calmly but firmly. 'This is as bad as it gets. The storm's directly overhead. That's good because it means it will be moving away soon.'

'I want to go back to England,' Beatrice sniffed.

'Where are you sailing to?'

'Damnation Island. I'm a mail-order bride.'

'That's something to look forward to, isn't it?' Adelaide reasoned. 'A new life in a new country?'

Beatrice sniffed. 'I wish I'd never come.'

Adelaide was mystified. 'Then why did you?'

'My fiancé jilted me. That was bad enough. But I lost the baby I was carrying. Seven months gone I was, and she was still-born. I had nothing to look forward to, nothing to live for after that. So I signed up as a mail-order bride.'

'Don't you think you could grow to love your new husband?'

'I don't know.' She hiccupped. 'All I know is right now I'm scared, and I want my baby back. I just want to nurse her in my arms. Just once. But I can't, can I?'

'No, you can't,' agreed Adelaide. 'But you could certainly be useful and needed here on this trip.'

'But how? I've never done a day's work in my life. Not really. I was raised to be a wife and a mother. There's nothing much I can do 'cept play with babies.' She wiped her eyes. 'And men.' She gave an uncomfortable laugh. 'It's men that've always got me into trouble.'

'You had nothing to do with it, I suppose?'

Beatrice managed a smile. 'I could turn over a new leaf, I suppose. I'll have to when we arrive at Damnation anyway.'

'Why not turn one over now?'

'And miss all the fun?'

Adelaide raised an eyebrow.

Beatrice sighed. 'I suppose you could be right. And if I'm making myself useful I won't be able to get into any more trouble, will I?'

'Of course not.'

'The thing is I don't know what I can do that would be useful.'

'The first thing is to return to your cabin and tidy your hair. You'll feel much better. Then come back here as fast as you can and help me. I'll find you plenty to do.'

And stop your clinging onto Luke like he's your last hope of salvation, thought Adelaide.

* * * * *

Back in her cramped and dingy cabin, Beatrice scrambled among the clothes strewn on the floor and finally retrieved her silver-backed hairbrush. She toweled her hair dry and brushed it till it shone. Then she applied a light coating of face powder and lipstick. Adelaide had been right. She felt better already. She changed into a clean skirt and jumper and started for the door to join her new friend. She glanced at her cabin. There was not one inch that wasn't covered by discarded clothing. She could tidy it up, just for appearances sake but wasn't quite sure where to begin. So she pushed everything under the bed and headed out of her cabin towards the sickbay. She was on a journey to a new life, and who knew what might come of it?

* * * * *

The bare light bulb in the sickbay swung and swayed precariously from its cord, casting dark shadows here, illuminating a grey face there.

Adelaide had sorted the patients waiting to see the doctor into two groups —those with seasickness and minor injuries in one queue, the ones who appeared to have something more seriously wrong with them into another group. Already the doctor had almost finished with the second group and was ready to turn his attention to the ones who were merely seasick.

* * * * *

When Beatrice returned, her hair dry and combed, her face made up, Adeleide looked at her radically changed appearance and suddenly recognized her. This was the same woman who'd flirted so outrageously with the sailors when they'd embarked. Still, an extra pair of hands was always useful.

'What can I do?' asked Beatrice.

'Help me with the sick-bags.'

Quickly they moved from patient to patient, Adelaide delivering new bags and a reassuring word as she went, Beatrice taking away the used ones and the doctor coming behind both of them with seasickness remedies. About halfway down the line he said to Adelaide, 'We're short of medication. I don't think there'll be enough to go around.'

Adelaide thought a moment. 'I've got some powdered ginger in my cabin. That's supposed to be good when mixed with water. I'll go and fetch it.' It was time she checked on Daniel anyway.

* * * * *

Beatrice's eyes lit up in delight when Adelaide returned to the sickbay, Daniel crying lustily over one shoulder and small sachets of powdered ginger in her hands.

'You've got a baby! You lucky thing. May I have a look?'

'You can cuddle him.' Adelaide handed her infant to Beatrice who immediately held out her arms to hold him. 'He's called Daniel.'

'The lion-tamer.' Beatrice smiled. 'What happened to his father?'

'He died.'

'I'm so sorry, Adelaide. Here I was feeling sorry for myself, thinking you had everything.' At that moment Daniel began to cry lustily. 'You'd better take him back —I think he wants a feed.'

As Beatrice handed Daniel back Adelaide heard the tinge of regret in her voice, noticed the two large damp patches appear and spread across the front of Beatrice's blouse. Beatrice looked down. 'Yes, that still happens when a baby cries,' she said matter-of-factly. 'Well I'll make myself useful. If you can get on with your life after your husband died, I'd better get along with mine.'

As she sat on an upright chair nursing her infant, Adelaide watched Beatrice working with the unwell passengers, plumping up a pillow here, straightening a sheet there. Although she herself was capable, Beatrice seemed to have a gift for nursing. And she appeared to have a particular aptitude with children. As the young woman disappeared from her range of vision, a germ of an idea was born inside Adelaide's head. Daniel had almost finished feeding, when Adelaide sensed rather than heard the ship's engines fall silent. And because the vessel was no longer ploughing through the water, the up and down movement of the waves seemed more exaggerated than before.

She cuddled Daniel closer, hoping Beatrice hadn't noticed the silence. Another display of nerves was the last thing they all needed.

At that moment Luke came into the sickbay, his face haggard. He was half-helping, half-carrying an elderly man and addressed the doctor. 'He fell out of his bunk and hurt his arm, doc. I think it's just bruised, but I'd like you to check him over.'

'What's wrong, Luke?' whispered Adelaide as the doctor took over from Luke and tended the elderly man.

'Someone's missing. We've searched all over and can't find her, so we think she may have fallen overboard. It's almost light. If we don't find her we'll have to go back and look for her.'

'Luke, that's dreadful.'

Luke shrugged, 'It happens from time to time. But on a passenger ship it's not good.'

'Who is it who's missing?'

'One of the mail-order brides. You might remember her —the men were around her like bears around a honey-pot. She was stunning. A real beauty. Everyone was after a piece of the action.'

An unwelcome stab of jealousy knifed through her. So Luke had noticed her too. Angrily she bit her lip. She shouldn't feel possessive of Luke, of his affections, when she herself was already married. But she just couldn't help it. If Luke liked Beatrice it would be one less complication in her own life. One less thing to take her mind off her new husband, making her new life simpler. And easier.

'Relax, Luke,' she said, 'she's here. You brought her in yourself.'

Shock wiped all the expression from Luke's face. 'When?'

'She was the hysterical woman you brought in earlier. The one who was scared witless.'

'Are you sure?'

'Certain. She's around here somewhere. Doing a bit of nursing.'

'But she didn't look like the same woman!'

'She was frightened, Luke, that's all. I gave her something useful to do. I think we need a nursery on board, and Beatrice is just the person to run it.'

The etched lines of worry on Luke's face were suddenly ironed smooth. 'Adelaide, you're brilliant!'

'Nothing your average pioneering woman wouldn't do.'

'You're not an average pioneering woman, though, are you?'

Adelaide blushed. A nice compliment. But she didn't want to hear it. She was on her way to safety with Daniel. To make a fresh start with her new husband. She didn't need the further complication of feelings for a man with whom there was no future. Did she?

* * * * *

In the blackness of his cabin Luke Collins lay tossing and turning on his bunk. He'd had a hard forty-eight hours with the storm and the cleaning up of the ship afterwards. He should have been able to sleep. Instead he was wide awake, thoughts chasing themselves through his head. James Rawtenstall had told him Adelaide was an unbalanced, selfish and spoilt woman who had deliberately caused her own husband's death. That simply didn't stack up against his own observations. He'd had James Rawtenstall's version. Now somehow he had to get Adelaide's.

* * * * *

In the stillness of the night Adelaide gave up trying to sleep. Carefully she extricated her limbs from the warmth of the blankets, turned on the bedside lamp and once again read the note that had been slipped under her door. Handwritten, it had been addressed to no-one in particular. Nor was there any signature. It read simply, 'Run as far as you can. You'll never be able to hide.'

The old fear she'd almost let go of returned. She was cornered, trapped. Her escape plans could come to nothing. James Rawtenstall had sent someone after her, and they knew exactly where she was. There was no possibility of jumping ship. And probably little possibility of her getting ashore on Damnation Island. She could trust no-one, except maybe Luke. But that would mean telling him her secret, and she couldn't do that. It was unfair to drag him into her personal battles. Of course she could choose to ignore the note, but that would mean running away from her problems. She'd never done that, and she wasn't about to start. She could take the note to the ship's captain, outline her position and ask for his help. But she'd booked her passage under an alias, and there would be no telling if he would react favorably or unfavorably to her predicament.

She'd mix first with the passengers, then with the crew. She'd keep her mouth shut, her eyes and ears open, searching for snippets of information from anyone who'd had any dealings with James Rawtenstall. It would take time, of course, and she'd have to be thorough.

Finally satisfied with this decision, she drifted into sleep, only to be jolted wide awake again. If James Rawtenstall had paid someone to follow her, he or she would be unlikely to let drop any verbal clues, since the transaction would be a financial one, not an emotional one. The only thing she could do would be to wait and see if there was anyone to stop her disembarking on Damnation Island.

Outside the porthole dawn cracked the sky, opening it gradually to the coming day. Inside the cabin tears of frustrated helplessness seeped slowly from the corners of Adelaide's eyes, dripping onto the pillow beneath her, bringing the sleep of the exhausted and the damned.

CHAPTER SEVEN

It was a quiet rap on the cabin door that aroused Adelaide from her troubled lethargy. Let them knock, she thought dully, I don't have to open it to anyone.

'Adelaide, are you all right?'

Luke!

Relief flooded through her as she crawled out of bed, pulled on a dressing-gown and cracked the door open slightly.

His eyes were laughing as he said, 'The Captain's announced a dance tonight. Will you...?' He stopped. 'Whatever's wrong?'

'Nothing.' she replied flatly, memories of the note dulling her pleasure at seeing Luke.

'Yes there is.' He pushed open the cabin door and crossed the threshold. 'And I'm not leaving till you tell me what it is.'

'I'm just tired.'

'It's more than that.'

Adelaide thought quickly. 'I'm feeling a little homesick, that's all.'

Luke's eyes watched her intently. 'I don't believe you've got a weak bone in your body. Try something else.' He sat on the arm of a chair. 'I've got all the time in the world. And I intend to use it. Let's start at the beginning, shall we?'

'What do you mean?'

'Adelaide, you booked your passage under the name of Margaret Aspinall. You gave your name to Beatrice as Adelaide

Rawtenstall. You showed no reaction when I called you Adelaide. That's your real name, isn't it?

Adelaide nodded silently.

'Adelaide, we're more than friends. We're a team. And a good one. Can't you tell me what you're running from?'

Adelaide was in turmoil. She wanted to tell Luke, share her secret. But she couldn't risk losing Daniel. Her burden was too great. She shook her head. 'No Luke, I can't. Please don't ask me again.'

'All right, I'll do as you wish.' His tone became firm. 'But tell me what has upset you so recently.'

Adelaide had no alternative. She walked into the bedroom, picked up the note from the floor and returning to the sitting room, handed it to him. 'I received this yesterday.'

Luke's face darkened as he read it. 'Stay here. I know this handwriting.'

As he went out he slammed the door with a force that shook the cabin walls.

* * * * *

By late afternoon all debris from the storm had been cleared, and preparations were well underway for the captain's ball, to be given to celebrate the storm's passing.

Adelaide had set up a nursery with Beatrice supervising the children and was quietly pleased to see how well the other woman took charge. All she'd needed was direction and a little encouragement, and this capable, confident, young woman was almost unrecognizable as the tease who had flirted so outrageously with the sailors at embarkation.

Adelaide left the nursery and returned to her cabin. She quickly stripped off her outer clothes and her underwear and entered the shower. The cascade of warm water soothed her soul and her spirit, and as she shampooed her long hair, rinsing its thickness beneath the showerhead, she gave thanks to the heavens for allowing her the joy of Luke's company, the satisfaction of seeing Beatrice's transformation from dizzy blonde to confident young woman. When she was finished she toweled herself dry. Then she slipped her arms through the sleeves of her bathrobe, tied it at the waist and wrapped a towel around her wet hair. She stepped out of the bathroom, through her bedroom and into the sitting room. To her surprise Beatrice was sitting in one of the easy chairs.

'I owe you, Adelaide.' Beatrice smiled warmly. 'So I'm babysitting while you're at the ball.' She walked into the bedroom and opened Adelaide's wardrobe. 'Wear this,' she said, taking out a long silk dress of deep sapphire blue, trimmed around the cleavage with black lace. 'It matches your eyes. May I do your hair? I'm quite good at it.'

Sitting at the dressing-table, Adelaide smiled. This was the kind of thing her sisters would have shared with her. How she missed them. She watched in the mirror as Beatrice's hands moved through her hair, pulling a piece up here, a strand down there, clipping and holding them in place with diamante pins to show off her high cheekbones. Then she brushed the dark tresses over her neck and shoulders in a cascading torrent of ebony warmth.

'He'll love you like this!'

Adelaide met Beatrice's eyes in the mirror. 'Who will?' she asked steadily.

'Don't tell me you haven't noticed! Luke Collins, of course. Who else?'

Adelaide blushed, laughing uncertainly. 'Beatrice, there's nothing between Luke Collins and me.' Not yet, anyway.

Beatrice persisted, meeting Adelaide's eyes in the mirror. 'Surely you've seen how he looks at you, watches your every move? He never takes his eyes off you. A widow needs a bit of fun now and then, Adelaide. You've been good to me and to the other passengers. Go out and enjoy yourself —if not for your own sake, then for mine. Opportunity —of the right kind —is knocking at your door, if only you could see it. Think of it as one for the road!'

'Why don't you come to the ball, Beatrice? You could have one for the road yourself!'

'No thanks. I've turned over a new leaf. I'll enjoy sitting with Daniel. Helps me get over my own little one. And don't worry,' she added, 'I won't forget to give him back!'

* * * * *

In the ballroom displays of fresh fruit were piled into colorful centrepieces on the tables. Crystal decanters, brimful of red and white wines sparkled in the reflected light from the candelabras overhead. A five-piece orchestra played softly in the background. Adelaide's hand was tucked snugly into Luke's arm as they were shown to their places at the captain's table. Everywhere women were wearing their best dresses —some long, others short. The men were a mixed bunch, some in suits, the occasional one in a dinner-jacket, some dressed the part as sailors, with thick Aran sweaters and sailor-hats. There was laughter and conversation, and the evening air crackled with anticipation of the night's entertainment to come.

She was glad she'd made the effort and come out. It would take her mind away from her worries about the note under the door. This was the one evening she would get to dance with Luke, be his dinner partner. There was no harm in it among all these people, was there?

The chef had excelled himself with roast lamb, vegetables and a mouthwatering gamut of luxurious desserts. Laughter tinkled through the ballroom as glasses were raised to each other and plates were cleared.

At the end of the meal the captain rose from his place at the head of the table. 'Ladies and gentlemen, I now propose a toast. To Luke Collins for safely bringing us around the Coast of Africa.'

The seamen stood, saluted and raised their glasses. 'To Luke Collins.'

Luke stood. 'Thank you. I now propose a second toast. To a wonderful helper, a woman who knows no fear. ' He raised his glass to his lips, his eyes meeting hers. 'Please rise and drink to Adelaide.'

Pride and embarrassment flushed through Adelaide as the crew and passengers stood as one. 'To Adelaide,' they replied in unison.

The band struck up the chords of 'For she's a jolly good fellow.'

Adelaide was bemused —both thrilled and embarrassed —and as the last strains of the song faded away, the band picked up the lilting melody of a waltz.

As if it were the most natural action in the world, Luke took her hand in his, led her on to the dance-floor and held her close. So close she could feel the movements of muscle and sinew in his strong, masculine body. As his hand rose from her waist up the small of her back, holding her, caressing her, they waltzed a path among the other dancers, Adelaide keeping absolute time with Luke, and it seemed to her that her feet barely touched the dance-floor.

'About that note under your door...' murmured Luke softly.

Immediately Adelaide tensed. She hadn't forgotten the note; she'd found a hiding place for it in the dark recesses of her mind. Now it was back on the surface, smugly reminding her that her life and freedom were not truly hers.

Luke continued. 'Apparently it was intended for Beatrice, from a love-sick sailor. It's been sorted out. Neither of you need to worry about it further.'

So it wasn't someone working for James Rawtenstall after all. Relief flooded through her, sending her light-headed with giddiness. 'Thank you.'

Almost imperceptibly, his arms tightened around her, pulling her gently against him, causing her silk-encased nipples to brush against his chest, making them harden. Adelaide could have kissed him she was so relieved, but the band saved her by changing tempo, this time with a lively tango.

As she danced, deeply aware of Luke, his closeness, his raw animal magnetism, Adelaide let go of her inhibitions, forgetting she was a married woman. When the dance ended, Luke took her by the arm, leading her out onto the deck to lean on the rails.

'Welcome to your first night in the tropics,' he said. 'Look straight above you.' In the balmy evening air Adelaide looked skywards. Spread above them like a velvet star-studded carpet was the Milky Way and behind it the bright glow of a lovers' moon.

Suddenly the sky lit up in front of them as a trail of silver streaked across the heavens, from one corner to the next.

'Some people call that a shooting star.' Luke's voice was husky behind her. 'I prefer the idea the people in the East have.'

He was so close it was as well she was turned away from him. She wanted him to hold her, wanted the touch of his strong arms around her, the feel of his heart pounding in his chest. Her voice snagged in her throat. 'What idea is that?'

'They believe they are magic carpets. If you ride one, you are granted a very special wish. Wish now, Adelaide, wish with all your heart, and it will come true.'

Adelaide closed her eyes. God help her, because she couldn't help herself. There was only one thing she yearned for. She inhaled deeply, the musky smell of aroused male in her nostrils, wanting to taste him, to touch him. Against her better judgment she wished Luke Collins in her life forever.

It was done. She shivered.

'Cold?' His deep voice caressed her lobes, his hands rested gently but firmly on her shoulders, sending rivulets of anticipation through her body.

'Not really. It's just so...lovely here. I could sail all my life.'

'Tell me what you want from life, for yourself.'

She knew very well what she wanted now. But she couldn't, wouldn't say. 'I'd like to go to Egypt, plod and sway on camel back across the desert, see the pyramids.'

'I'd be with you. We'd race to the pyramids, encircle them and stop at an oasis.'

'You make it sound like fun. And what would we do there?'

Luke's tone grew serious. 'I'd spread a bright blanket under a palm tree for you to lie on. I'd lift you down from your camel, carry you to the water, wash the dust from your feet and lay you down on the blanket.'

'You think so?'

'I know so.' His breath fanned her cheek as he moved closer to her. 'I'd climb the nearest date palm and swing down with an armful of dates and feed them to you one by one.' Adelaide's heart skipped a beat. This was the first time Luke had mentioned them doing anything as a couple. Oh, it was wonderful to have someone to dream with.

'Really?'

'Certainly. When we were both refreshed, I'd mount you on my camel, and we'd ride together towards one of the souks.' His hands moved from her shoulders, down her back to her waist, where he held her tenderly. 'I'd buy you trinkets, gold bangles for your wrists and ankles.'

'And no doubt a ruby for my navel?'

'The brightest, most exquisite ruby the western world had ever seen. And even that would pale into insignificance compared to your great physical beauty, the goodness and loveliness of your soul.'

She could feel his eyes seeking hers, knew she mustn't gaze into them, or she would be lost. She looked away and studied his sculpted lips, the slight cleft in his chin.

'You flatter me too much, Luke.'

'I speak only the truth.'

'What if I said I'd like to go to the jungle?' Adelaide asked in an attempt to lighten the growing tension.

'I'd be there by your side. I'd row your canoe up the River Congo.'

'Maybe I could row myself.'

Luke's face grew serious, his tone firm. 'But you'd need a master to steer you. To keep you in line, away from crocodiles and hippos. Or any other animals. I'd do that while I rowed you. And you'd be able to see the jungle animals at times; you'd watch the zebras and giraffes as they graze the plains.'

'You know your way around, don't you?'

'Certainly. I'd be your teacher and your guide. You'd want for nothing. You'd see the world through a different set of eyes, like you've never seen it before. And at night, we'd camp. I'd pitch your tent, build a fire, shoot some game and cook it. It would be the sweetest dish you'd ever tasted.'

'Oh, Luke, that's so...'

'Romantic?'

'Yes.'

'And so it's intended to be. You deserve nothing but the best. Adelaide, in the time we've spent together I've had the chance to observe your compassion with the sick and the frightened. I've seen the way you help others. At times you must have been frightened, yet you never let it show. We'd make a great team, Adelaide. I'd always look out for you, and you'd come to no harm. But more than that —'

Panic stricken, she realized she couldn't let him go any further. For both their sakes. She interrupted quickly. 'Tell me what you'd do if we went to the Antarctic!'

'I'd teach you how to fish from a boat, how to steer a ship between the icebergs, how to listen to the creaking and cracking of the ice and how to understand what it means.'

'It'd be cold, Luke.'

'Not with me around, it wouldn't be. Believe me, you wouldn't feel the cold.'

'Not even in the Antarctic?'

'I'd keep your bed so hot at night the afterglow would stay with you all during the next day.'

'And if I simply wanted to go home to England?'

Luke wasn't playing a game now. This was real. Tenderly, he lifted his hands to her cheeks, cupped her face. 'I'd take you back by whichever route you chose.'

Adelaide tilted her head back slightly, unknowingly raising her lips to his, her Paris-night eyes meeting his smoldering grey ones. They were so close she could feel his breath mingle with hers. Unconsciously she raised her hand to his chest, feeling his heartbeat quicken beneath her moist fingers. Trembling she half-whispered, 'Oh, Luke...'

Luke bent his head, his mouth taking hers without warning, hard and fast, breathing his life force into her spirit. His arms came around her as he pulled her towards him, welding their bodies together.

From a long way off Adelaide heard the orchestra playing some slow song or dance. She didn't care what it was. All that mattered was that she was in Luke's arms, responding to his embrace, holding him in hers. Luke pressed her against the rail, his manhood hard against her belly. Her breath quickened, caught, and deep in her throat a moan started. Her hands raked his hair, thick to her touch as his hands caressed her waist, the flare of her hips. His lips slid across her cheek to kiss her hairline, then he sighed against her ear as he fought to regain control. But the softness and scent of her drew him on, his mouth developing a will of its own, moving down her neck to the firmness of her collarbone.

His shaking hands cupped her breasts, which were peaked beneath her silk bodice, straining for freedom. His thigh parted hers, and Adelaide felt a deep longing surge upwards through her body. Yearned for him to knead the dull throb that had become part of her. His lips brushed the top of her cleavage, no longer gentle but urgent, demanding as his tongue laved her silky bodice, teasing the nipples beneath, biting gently, causing a soft moan to feather out from between her lips.

She was aware only of his corded arms as he swiftly gathered her into his arms and holding her close to his chest, carried her down a deserted stairway.

*****

Luke's cabin was dimly lit, the lamps throwing a soft glow of warmth around the small room. Adelaide had time only to feel her feet gently touch the floor before Luke pushed her up against the door, his hands shaking as he began to unpin her hair, letting it fall loose around her breasts.

'You're the most beautiful woman I've ever seen.' His voice was deep, caressing, and Adelaide could find no words, no desire, to halt the madness.

His hands shook as he unzipped her dress, freeing her rosy breasts, now peaked and hardened.

Her breathing came in short, soft gasps, as she unbuttoned his shirt to find a sprinkling of dark hair on his muscular chest. She pressed her hands to his chest, moved them to his back. Luke's breath came in harsh rasps. As her fingertips feathered his spine he groaned, urgently parting her thighs wider with his.

'Adelaide,' he groaned, his voice low, the guttural tone inflaming her soul. She stroked him gently, her hands pulling him closer.

Luke fought for control. He put his lips to Adelaide's shoulder, pausing as he almost gained supremacy. Adelaide put her head back and moaned softly, her body softening in his embrace. He tried to hold back, be gentle, but it was too late. He was lost.

With the primal ferocity of the jungle he lifted her into his arms, carried her to the bed and set her down among the pillows, as an animal savagery took over and his hands tore away her lacy panties. He stopped momentarily to free his bulging manhood.

Adelaide barely had time to raise her hips to meet his before he drove into her with such force and passion it took her breath away.

His mouth took hers hard and fast. He pulled her towards him, and, like a rosebud opening in the sunshine, her body burst into life.

Adelaide forgot to breathe as again and again he drove into her, taking her to the top of the waves of passion, never allowing her to crest them.

When she could stand no more and the cry started deep in her throat, he covered her mouth with his, groaning into her depths as his loins thrust into hers. He roared his triumph.

Finally spent, he held her in his arms, gently stroking her hair and murmured, 'Adelaide, I've wanted you from the first moment I met you.'

Sleepily Adelaide trailed a delinquent finger through the matted hairs of his chest, down his stomach, firm and taut as a washboard, to the blue-black hairs curled beneath, to his manhood and stroked. He stiffened at once.

'I was led to believe men needed to rest afterwards,' she smiled.

'Not the right man. Not when he's with the right woman. But this time I want to show you how much I love you.'

Slowly, patiently, with infinite cleverness, he brought her body to life again. Whispering tender words of endearment, he stroked her hair, kissed her eyelids, her nose, her breasts. His clever tongue laved her navel, and he encouraged her to explore him as he explored her.

Adelaide discovered an intimate courage she'd never known she possessed till Luke had awakened it. As they lay together, head to thigh, pleasuring each other, Adelaide discovered the rapture of giving, as well as receiving.

And when the rosy fingers of dawn crept through the cabin port-hole, when Adelaide didn't think she could possibly be more physically fulfilled or happier, Luke kissed her gently, once more awakening her senses to his, as he demanded entrance to her most secret parts.

'I love you, Adelaide. From the bottom of my soul and with all my heart.'

With his words she should have heard the sound of church bells pealing in joyous, welcoming celebration. Instead she heard the mournful tones of a death-knell in her heart, as she realized she hadn't told him she was one of the mail-order brides.

'Luke,' she murmured, trying to stop him before he went further, trying to save him from himself. 'Luke, there's something I must tell you.'

'Then say it. Let there be no secrets between us.'

'It's the reason I'm going to Damnation Island.'

Luke laughed, his voice rich, warm. 'A new beginning for a pioneering woman, right?'

'Yes, but —'

'You've got a baby.'

'Daniel.'

'You're a widow, right?'

'Yes, but —'

'No buts. I'll bring up Daniel as my son. We'll have more children – enough to start an orphanage if that's what you want.'

'It's more than that. I should have told you before but...'

A dark shadow flitted across his features. 'Just say it. You don't want a future with me.'

'Yes I do. But I'm a mail-order bride.'

The shadow disappeared. 'Is that all? You haven't even met this man. All he's done is pay your passage. I can refund his money. Sail with me back to England, have the marriage annulled, and we'll get married properly. Man and wife we'll sail the world. I'll show you all the places we've talked about. We'll travel your beloved moors together. Then we'll return to all the best places with our children.'

Relief flooded through her. This was too good to be true. For once in her life, Adelaide was happy, at ease, as if nothing could hurt or disturb her any more. 'That would be wonderful, Luke. You don't mind?'

'Of course I mind my future wife being married to someone else.' He frowned. 'I knew there were mail-order brides on the ship —I just didn't realize you were one of them. But we'll attend to all that.'

A knock on the door disturbed them. 'Telegram!' shouted a voice on the other side of the door. Luke rose from the bed and covering himself with a towel, crossed the room and opened the door.

'Send room service with some champagne, please.' Luke said to the cabin boy as he took the telegram, read it briefly, crumpled it and let it fall to the floor. 'So you'll come back to England with me?'

'Yes Luke, I'll come back to England with you.'

CHAPTER EIGHT

Luke returned to the bed and gently, tenderly, with a sweetness that surprised and delighted them both, took her again.

When Adelaide awoke, languishing in the afterglow of their lovemaking, Luke had gone, presumably to keep watch or some other work on the ship. This was her Luke. The man she'd waited all her life for. The man she'd share her dreams with, have more children with, build a dynasty with. In the meantime she couldn't lie here all morning, and Daniel was still with Beatrice. Good as Beatrice was, she would be unable to feed him herself. Adelaide had left some milk with her the previous night, but Daniel would surely be ready for another feed by now. The only clothing she had with her, was the dress from last night. She'd put it back on and steal back to her cabin before anyone could see her and realize she'd spent the night 'out.' She was almost dressed when one of the nylon stockings she was putting on slipped from her hand and dropped to the floor. Bending to retrieve it, the draught from her silk dress caught the edge of the crumpled telegram, fluttering it around her feet like a mosquito. The signature 'James Rawtenstall' riveted her attention, holding it there, while goosebumps rose from her arms to the nape of her neck.

Her chest grew tight, her heart heavy and fearful as she stretched out a trembling hand to pick up the paper. She didn't want to read it, didn't want to destroy the joy, the togetherness of the past night. Luke had said there should be no secrets between them.

Hadn't he promised to care for Daniel as his own, promised them plenty of children, a life second to none? She could trust him. Couldn't she?

Tears blurred Adelaide's vision as she read the treacherous words. 'Congratulations on a job well done. By whatever means possible return my grandson and his mother to me. Ten thousand pounds for you when you return with them. Regards, James Rawtenstall.'

The page seared her fingertips like a live coal. Adelaide dropped it and wiped her hands down her skirts, as if she could wipe away the disgust she felt, for herself, Luke and James Rawtenstall. Icy fingers of shame clawed across her scalp, down her neck, to cover her body in goosebumps. She'd been duped by Luke, and fool that she was, she'd played straight into James Rawtenstall's hands. She couldn't have made it any easier for either of them. She should have done what she intended at the outset —stayed in her cabin for the entire journey with Daniel. At the thought of her son her heart almost stopped. She needed to take him in her arms, feel his tiny body nestling into hers. She glanced at her watch. Daniel would be with Beatrice in the nursery by now.

She had to get to him before anyone else tried to.

Lifting her hem of her ballgown in her hands, she raced towards the nursery, threw the door open and heedless of the other mothers, snatched him from the nursery cot and sped down the corridor to her own cabin.

Only when she was sitting in an armchair, with Daniel sleeping in her arms, head snuggled against her breast, was she able to take stock of the situation. James Rawtenstall now knew exactly where she was. Her current position was thousands of miles away from England. She'd suspected he might try to find her, and he had. Therefore there was no surprise in that and no useful reason in allowing herself to become upset by it.

What shook her was Luke, how he'd obviously been planted to bring her back. Of course her father-in-law would have set up someone to find her. But Luke! How she would ever get over this affair she'd no idea. She loved him. She'd thought he loved her.

She'd ached to go back to England with him. All those dreams could come to nothing now. Her only future was on Damnation Island, with a stranger for a husband.

In the lonely cabin, Adelaide felt empty, drained of all emotion. Which was just as well, considering what had happened. Even if she'd wanted to cry she couldn't have. There were no more tears, no more emotions. Just a clinical analysis of her situation. Twice she'd been unlucky in love. She wouldn't be stupid enough to attempt it a third time. That was why her proxy marriage would work. It would be a business contract. And like any other contract it would work on logic and communication. It would offer shelter for herself and Daniel, and she would do her best at whatever wifely duty she was expected to perform. That way she wouldn't get hurt.

As the shadows lengthened, Adelaide still sat in the armchair, wearing the clothes she'd worn for the ball last night. From time to time Daniel fed, then slept, as if understanding her need for quiet. Eventually she changed him and put him to bed.

Nothing had passed Adelaide's lips. Not a morsel of food, not a drop of liquid. She needed nothing except sleep and copious amounts of water. Breastfeeding made her thirsty, and she'd neglected herself these last hours. She took off her ball-gown and stuffed it into the waste-bin. Then her undergarments. They also went into the waste-bin. She wouldn't wear them again —any of them. She certainly never wanted to see them, ever. She showered, washing traces of Luke from her body, and pulled on an old cotton nightgown. Plain and practical. That's how things would be from now on. She was so deep in thought as she crossed the cabin towards the bedroom, she didn't hear her cabin door open and Luke stride in.

'You look beautiful!'

She wished she'd never seen the telegram. Never learned its contents. She needed nothing more than to be held in Luke's strong arms, to be loved and comforted. But the time for that was past.

'Take a good look. It's going to be your last.'

'Never, Adelaide.' He laughed. 'Your beautiful face is going to be the last thing I see before sleeping, the first vision upon awakening. I'll have the warmth of your body in my arms, your silken hair on my chest, your legs entwined with mine, inviting, satisfied.'

'Save your words, Luke. Save them for my father-in-law, James Rawtenstall.'

Luke stopped in his tracks. He should have explained things before now, clarified his position and asked about hers directly to get her side of the story. Now it might be too late. 'You read the telegram.'

'You were working for him all the time, weren't you?'

'Yes —'

'And you both thought you had me nicely sewn up, no doubt?'

'No. I was to look out for you. To make sure no harm befell you.'

'Really? And what about returning me to England?'

'I was to do that if that was what you wanted.'

'I played very neatly into your hands, didn't I?'

'No. Adelaide —'

'I fell into your arms and your bed. Like a bitch in heat. James Rawtenstall will LOVE that one!'

Luke took her in his arms. She shook herself free.

'Adelaide, listen to me. James Rawtenstall brought tremendous pressure to bear. If I hadn't done as he asked my mother and sisters would have been thrown out of their home. They live in one of his cottages. I couldn't allow that. But I fell in love with you the moment I met you. I wanted to hear your version of things. Then matters got out of ... control, as you know.'

'What did you want of me?'

'I wanted, and still want, you to become my wife.'

These were the words Adelaide wanted to hear. Her heart cried out in anguish. In any other circumstances it would have been wonderful. But not this way. Never.

He continued. 'You mean so much to me, Adelaide. And I know you have feelings for me.'

Adelaide looked away. 'You love me? Did you know I was James Rawtenstall's daughter-in-law?'

'Of course I knew. That made no difference.' He took her in his arms, held her close. 'Adelaide, you've enchanted me.'

It felt so good. She wanted to stay there, wanting above all else to be in his arms forever. Her skin was on fire from Luke's touch. She had to break free.

'Consider the spell of enchantment broken.' She struggled out of his arms. 'For both of us. I never want to lay eyes on you again.' Adelaide turned away, hiding her tears as she did so. 'I don't want to have you near me.'

Luke took a step towards Adelaide, put his arms on her shoulders. 'Adelaide, we were meant for each other. I can't live without you. You can't live without me.'

'We'll both have to learn, won't we? I no longer want to think of you. I don't want you in my dreams.'

'But I will be, Adelaide, as you will be in mine. Always.' He tightened his hands on her shoulders. 'We can't escape that. Nor can we escape what we had and could have had. I love you, Adelaide. Go, if you must – I'll not stop you. But I'll be back. For you. And when I return I won't take no for an answer.'

'Luke, it's not possible.'

'Adelaide...we've been together on this trip. We've laughed and we've loved. We both know that whoever else we meet, nothing could touch what we've had, not even come close. I was serious when I said I wanted to marry you.'

'That can never be, Luke.'

'Yes, Adelaide. It can be.'

Adelaide sighed. Luke was everything she had ever wanted in a man. She loved him with all her heart and her soul.

'I couldn't...trust you ever again.'

'Yes you can.'

'I don't trust you now.'

Luke thought quickly. Adelaide was right. She couldn't trust him now. He couldn't blame her for that, given her circumstances. He needed to prove himself with actions, not words, if he was to get anywhere. It was a long shot, but worth it. Another plan formulated in his mind.

'If that's your choice, I have no option but to accept it. But only for the moment. There's something else I would like to share with you – one last thing —before we go our separate ways.'

'And what would that be?'

'Will you trust me?'

'Trust you? Luke, I've already trusted you, and you've betrayed me. How could I possibly trust you again?'

'Just on this one occasion. It won't be difficult, I promise you. There's nothing to fear.'

'You mean there's no more to fear after you've betrayed me to James Rawtenstall?'

'No, that wasn't what I meant.' He turned her round to face him. 'Adelaide, nothing and nobody can take away from us what we have already had. But I've something to show you.'

'It had better be good. And it won't make me change my mind.'

'Come with me to the crow's nest.'

'You've got to be joking!'

'Please.' Luke 's tone was serious. Adelaide looked into his eyes, wanted to fall into their depths, wanted him to hold her and kiss away all her fears. But she couldn't do it. She couldn't allow herself to fall under his charms again.

'No.'

'Just once more, I beg you.'

Adelaide saw the anguish in his eyes. Could he really have been as much a pawn in James Rawtenstall's game as she had been?

'I trusted you...' Adelaide whispered as she choked back the tears that threatened to engulf her.

'And you can trust me again. Adelaide, I'm not going to tell you how much I love you.' Luke tightened his arms around her, holding her close. 'I've done that. I'm not going to ask you to marry me again.'

All around her was silence, save for the lapping of the waves against the bow of the ship. 'There's something I want you to see.' His voice was ragged. 'I've already promised you free and safe return to England.'

'Luke, you know I can't take up your offer.'

'If I promise to deliver you safely to Damnation, will you come with me to the crow's nest — for one last time?'

He sensed her hesitation and remained silent.

'Do you promise not to try to make me change my mind?'

'It'll cost me dearly, but if that's what you really want, you've got my promise.'

Adelaide thought hard. This would be her final time with Luke. She would take the time and treasure it.

'All right, Luke. You win. Tomorrow morning?'

Luke smiled and kissed her hand. 'I'll collect you up at dawn.'

* * * * *

The skies were clear, and the breeze fresh the next morning as Adelaide and Luke climbed the ratlines for the second time. It was easier this time. As before Luke was behind her to catch her should she fall. The only reason she'd agreed to come was the fact that she enjoyed the thrill of the climb. It would be her last time. All feelings for Luke, good and bad, were blessedly gone. At some point she'd have to deal with them, she knew that, but not now. And while she could neither forgive nor forget, the rational part of her knew there was a lot of good in him. She'd take her memories, maybe hold them close from time to time. But for now she'd enjoy herself. After all, she was only eighteen.

Finally they reached the tiny platform. She didn't need Luke's help now. She braced herself against the wind. Below them, the waters of the South Atlantic were transformed from funereal grey to a definitive navy.

'Look there,' said Luke, pointing to the left. 'See anything?'

'Not yet,' said Adelaide. 'There's nothing, except a mound of white cloud.'

'That's Damnation Island,' said Luke, behind her. 'Most times it's hidden by cloud. When it lifts, you'll see your new homeland.' His voice roughened. 'Close your eyes.'

Adelaide closed them. Something cold and metallic touched her skin, lay languorously around her neck. The bare flesh of her nape cooled momentarily as she felt Luke lift her heavy mane of hair, heard the metallic 'snap' of a clasp being shut.

'Touch it whenever you wish. Admire it in a mirror as often as you please. For the rest of your life it's locked on, and I've got the key.

He held out his hand. Dwarfed by his palm, an ornate curlicued key glistened in a shaft of morning sunlight.

'This pendant goes from one generation of Collins women to the next. It's yours now.' He drew back his arm and flung the key into the air, far from the crow's nest, where it landed without a ripple in the ocean.

Adelaide moved her fingers to the pendant. It felt warm and smooth. A gift from Luke, it was comfortable in her fingers.

'Luke, I can't accept this,' she said in a low voice.

'You already have. It's an emerald pendant, a reminder that I'll be back. And next time I won't take 'no' for an answer.

'I'm married, Luke. And you work for James Rawtenstall.'

'So you say. It's principles and ethics that have driven us apart, not lack of love. I'm not giving up. You're going to be mine, whatever you may think. If we do the right thing, neither of us will miss out. You'll see.' His tone was firm, his facial expression bereft.

Her heart remained stony, cold, unfeeling. But she put her fingers around the ornament for comfort. She'd keep it as a spoil of war. A memento of what could have, should have been.

She couldn't trust herself to speak. She merely nodded and started back down the ratlines to her new life.

CHAPTER NINE

The morning was cold and gray, enjoyed only by the seagulls that followed the ship as it ploughed its relentless way towards Damnation Island.

Adelaide leaned into the rails on the ship's deck, her eyes closed against the miserable day before them. But she was unable to blot the misery from her soul. She thrust her hands into the sleeves of her jumper, searching for warmth and solace. There was none.

When she'd left England Adelaide had imagined she'd said all her goodbyes. She knew now she couldn't have been more wrong. She opened her eyes and watched her shadow on the deck as the cold fingers of dawn circled her heart and soul. She closed them again and shuddered. Already the blessed numbness that had descended upon her like a blanket, protecting her from the ravages of her emotions, was beginning to melt. The cold sinews of reality began to squeeze, freezing out any hope for her future happiness. Despite the pendant, despite all his assurances to the contrary, Luke was out of her life. He'd unlocked the gateway to her heart, promising warmth and love, affection and growth. Now it was slammed firmly shut. It wouldn't be opened again. Not by Luke, not by anyone. She'd had too many betrayals to believe otherwise. She'd just take every hour as it came and do her best for Daniel with no hopes or aspirations for the future.

When she re-opened her eyes, land was ahead, rising before her like a giant bird of prey. Menacing and dark, it brooded across the ocean, challenging any sea-vessel to attempt a landing. The mountaintop was shrouded in brown mist, hiding its secret ruminations. It was going to be a miserable and desolate eighteen years. She shuddered again and turned to go below decks.

*****

Inside the cabin Adelaide had a last look around. She didn't allow her eyes to rest on the easy chairs where she and Luke had talked, exploring each other's ideas, sharing their plans. When she went into the bedroom she didn't allow her glance to linger on the pillow where she'd dared to dream of a future for herself and Luke, where for a brief passage of time she'd allowed herself to believe it could be possible. Her cabin trunk was packed. She left her black hair to flow loosely around her shoulders. She couldn't bring herself to dress it, so great was her sorrow. Daniel had been nursed, dressed and was lying on her bed, cooing softly to himself. Silently she lifted his tiny, warm body into her circle of her arms, checked to make sure she'd left nothing behind —other than hopes, dreams and a shattered heart —and walked out, slamming the door behind her.

When she finally climbed onto the deck, she found it full of passengers dressed in warm, bright clothing, chattering and laughing excitedly in the emerging sunshine, many of them pointing towards the island as the ship moved closer to her new home.

Damnation Island was much nearer than before. Even from the ship, crevasses were visible in the rock-face, black and deep like the sorrow in her heart. The island had protected itself with a wide mat of thick seaweed, preventing the ship from approaching any closer. It had learned its lesson from her own heart. And where did that leave her proxy husband? Exactly where he was when she had first left England. He'd get what he'd bought —a mail-order bride. No less and certainly no more. She'd allow herself a nodding acquaintanceship with emotional intimacy in the future. That was all. It would have to be enough.

Adelaide's ears vibrated as the anchors rumbled their descent on their heavy chains. Now they were closer; small insets of emerald velvet grass became visible at the base of the rock. At least the island was fertile, with room for growth and nourishment, where beauty could blossom.

Maybe, given time, she could learn from the island and construct a new life for herself and Daniel. Maybe.

CHAPTER TEN

On Damnation Island, several outlying cottages crouched on a bleak headland overlooking the ocean. A path, no more than a grassy track, led further to a solitary cottage. It was different from the others in that its stones were whitewashed rather than weatherbeaten. Red shutters hugged the windows. Beneath their sills hung window-boxes overflowing with brightly-colored flowers. Above the chimney of the thatched roof a feather of smoke plumed upwards.

Inside his home John Maggott pulled on his best work trousers, rippled his sinewy arms and torso into a woolen shirt and critically appraised the master bedroom.

He'd built the large four-poster bed himself, spending long hours carving patterns on the wood, oiling it and finally polishing it till even he was pleased with the result. His new wife could change the curtains if she wished. That would be her prerogative.

He strode into the bathroom where an array of perfumes and bath oils were displayed for her on the windowsill. Fresh towels, pink and blue and edged in satin hung on the rails. He hoped she'd be pleased with these two rooms.

The church bells pealed a welcome across Thunder Bay as was the custom whenever a ship breached the horizon. There was plenty of time yet. He crossed through the parlor, whistling as he went. Then he stopped and picked up his Bible from the table and replaced it in the vacant section on the shelf above the hearth. He read it often, drew comfort from it, but his wife might not necessarily read it. Again that was her prerogative.

The nook by the fire was filled with shelves each one of them heavy with books. If she was a reader —and he hoped she would be —there was something here to suit all tastes. His eyes scanned his collection, his pride and joy, accumulated over the years from passing ships and sometimes ordered from overseas. On each side of the hearth was an armchair where he hoped they could sit and talk.

His footsteps echoed as he crossed the kitchen's wooden floor. He turned the morning's hot bread onto cooling wires and placed a casserole of fish and vegetable stew into the oven. She could rearrange the kitchen —indeed the whole house —if she wished. A woman's touch was what was needed here his friends had always said, and he had to agree with them. One last look around. Everything was in order. As much order as he could manage.

He'd set two places at the table and as an after-thought placed a bowl of wild flowers in the middle. He was determined that this proxy marriage would get off to a good start, providing both of them with a satisfying life. He hoped she'd like it. It was the best he could do.

* * * * *

In the depths of the South Atlantic Ocean the tectonic plates shifted again. Not a minor cough this time —this was a belly-rumbling belch that rippled an extra wave to the surface. Out of rhythm with the other waves, it moved inexorably in the direction of Damnation Island.

* * * * *

John Maggott opened the back door and started down the path, his spirits rising as they always did whenever he went outdoors.

He was a fortunate man. He worked hard and had a comfortable life on Damnation Island, a pleasant home, the warm friendships of good friends and interesting books. The only thing missing was a wife, and he'd always wanted his own children. Women were in short supply on Damnation. But that wasn't the real reason he'd remained unmarried. He'd wanted a woman with vision, someone who knew something of the outside world. It would be better for his children if they knew something other than island life. So he had opted for a mail-order bride. An unknown quantity and a risk. But one he was prepared to take.

Naturally he'd taken the precaution of making up a bed in one of the spare rooms, just in case of a major disaster. Like his new wife having two heads or something like that. If things seemed immediately as if they wouldn't work out, she wouldn't be sharing his bed, though he resolved to do his best to see that didn't happen. A highly sensual man, he wanted as fulfilling a married life as he could get.

He planned for them to take their time to get to know each other. He wanted to climb the Peak, go walking, fishing, dancing with her. And maybe sing. John had the best tenor voice on the island. If his wife could sing or even play the accordion, they could make a stunning double-act. He also wanted lots of children. And have them he would.

His feet left imprints in the sandy earth as he moved swiftly down the track towards the landing beach at Thunder Bay. It was a source of pleasure and pride to him that he was known as the fastest man on the island. He hoped any son of his would carry on the title. In the meantime he'd have to adjust his stride to suit his new wife, as he did with other people on the island.

Within five minutes —and it would have taken anyone else twenty —he joined the first of his friends and neighbors as they waited for the women to land on the beach. The ship had anchored off-shore as ships had to when the seaweed lay thick and silent around the island.

The welcoming party was starting to assemble on the beach with gifts for the new brides —some traditional offerings of fresh vegetables and fruit, some small presents for the household. He hoped his own gifts of feminine bathroom lotions would be well accepted. He hopped across the rocks to the line of rowing boats that was used to ferry passengers and mail from the ships on days like this.

'Eager to meet your wife, John?' called one of the other men.

'Yes,' he replied amiably, 'and she'd better be fertile!'

A series of loud guffaws broke from the circle of waiting men 'That's it, John, if she's ugly as sin she's still yours!'

'They're all beautiful when the lights're out!' he laughed back.

CHAPTER ELEVEN

As the small craft dipped and swayed across the seaweed, Adelaide sat on the front bench of the rowing boat, Daniel in her arms, her heart heavy, straining in her chest as it struggled to circulate the blood around her body in time with the gentle plop-whoosh-plop of the oars as they propelled the boat through the water. She breathed in, reminding herself not to forget to breathe out again.

The emotional shock of loving and leaving Luke was seeping through her pores, leaving her in the clutches of an almost depressive stupor so —unlike the other women —she didn't wave to the ship's crew as she traveled the final journey to her new home.

The love of her life was lost, not to war like her husband, not to illness like her family. He was lost because they'd both been pawns in James Rawtenstall's chess game.

The time for being a pawn in anyone's game was now up. She couldn't hope to grow to love her new husband. Not after Luke. It was unthinkable. But she would keep house for him, cook for him, maybe eventually bear his children. She could even work at being a good and pleasant companion. It was a business deal. She was what he'd bought. She'd never love again, she knew that as surely as she knew night follows day. But that wasn't a bad thing. She'd have a place of safety for herself and Daniel. Without emotion she couldn't get hurt. Could she? Cordial relations with a decent, fair-minded husband would be a fair trade for the highs and troughs of love.

Wouldn't they?

She bit down hard on her lower lip, resolving not to falter in her determination.

In her arms Daniel stirred, opened his trusting blue eyes and smiled. A surge of maternal pride and love rushed through her, easing the tension in her muscles and soothing her tortured mind. She'd had her chance. She'd created her memories. She could now go forward, leaving Luke Collins and James Rawtenstall behind her. She'd spend her energies making a good life for herself and Daniel and put up with her new husband.

She didn't look back.

If she had she would have seen Luke, alone on the aft of the deck, watching her and Daniel until they had safely reached the island.

* * * * *

As the small craft slid to a halt in the shallows, Adelaide rose from her seat ready to set foot on Damnation Island. From behind them rushed a wave that almost toppled her into the water.

Not one person —passengers, crew, island dwellers —paid any heed to that wave. No one questioned it. They weren't to know that far below the ocean surface, the tectonic plates had shifted again, that the movement once started could not be stopped.

* * * * *

She'd never imagined it could have looked like this. She'd known it would be small, of course. She hadn't expected a busy harbor full of liners and tugboats as in the English ports she'd known, but she had anticipated at least a landing pier of some description. Instead there was nothing. Adelaide shivered. No wonder their fares had been paid for them.

The man closest to her, probably in his early forties, reached out strong arms and lifted Adelaide and Daniel over the water, and Adelaide put her first foot ashore.

After the weeks aboard ship, walking on solid ground was not as easy as she'd imagined it would be. Instead she found the movements of her feet were still making allowances for the movements of the ship in the water. Grateful for the assistance, she allowed herself to be helped across the rocks towards the beach, to her new home and her new husband.

'She's here! The first woman on shore! What's your name?'

'Adelaide Rawtenstall.'

'Arthur? Adelaide Rawtenstall is the first woman on shore!'

From the waiting crowd a cheer rose. Adelaide wasn't sure why. Maybe it was the customary greeting here. She hesitated, smiled and wiggled her fingers in a shy wave. Men, women and children waved back.

Adelaide looked about her. The landing-beach was bleak, desolate, and two distinct parties of people were forming. Original inhabitants and newcomers. A gentle breeze soughed through her hair, bringing to her face the smell of wet sand and rotting seaweed. Overhead, fishing birds wheeled noisily screaming and screeching as they came to land on the nearby rocks. A welcome or a warning? She couldn't tell. Around her the chatter and occasional nervous laugh of the other brides filled her ears. She glanced curiously in their direction.

'Come and pick your husband, Adelaide,' joked Beatrice, not unkindly. Adelaide stole a glance in the direction Beatrice was pointing.

In front of them a line of young men was forming. Every one of them handsome, tautly muscled and virile as they waited, hands clasped behind their backs, feet slightly apart, to claim their wives. The wind brought an older man shambling swiftly across the rocks to join the queue. His legs were so bandy they formed an almost perfect circle, and as his body flowed up and down like the fluid movements of the tide. Adelaide realized one leg must be shorter than the other. How he moved with such speed, despite his obvious physical impairment was a mystery. He must be very fit. His figure was asterisked by a thatch of orange-yellow hair. Neatly combed, it didn't attempt to conceal his eyes. While the right eye glanced to the heavens, the left trawled the earth, like a beetle combing for grubs. Poor man, Adelaide thought.

* * * * *

She estimated it took about an hour for all the women from the ship to assemble on the beach. One man who appeared to be in his forties stepped forward.

'Ladies,' he began, 'welcome home. I'm the headman. My name's Arthur Glass. You'll probably be tired after your journey, so I'll keep things brief. You've got twelve months to get to know your husbands, see if you can settle. If things don't work out you'll be free to return to England on the next boat.'

This was it. For better or for worse she was going to meet her new husband. The man who would provide a safe haven for herself and Daniel away from James Rawtenstall's awful vengeance.

The headman continued. 'After six months, there'll be a mass wedding here, with celebrations like you've never seen before.'

Adelaide wanted her man to be Luke Collins. Wanted to see him running across the rocky beach towards her, laughing into the wind, telling her it was all a dreadful mistake, that he was coming to take her as his wife. He'd said he'd come back. She wanted to believe him. But she knew that in reality that couldn't, wouldn't happen. He worked for James Rawtenstall. She'd have to make do with what she had, the bargain she'd bought into.

Her first duty was to Daniel. No one else.

Her eyes slid along the line of waiting testosterone. Each man was a specimen of coiled, virile manhood. No doubt the men acquired their strong musculature and superlative physique from outdoor labor every day of the year. It sat comfortably upon them. Given time she could probably do her wifely duty with any one of them. Not emotionally, but physically. Given time.

The headman's voice droned through her thoughts. 'We all welcome you and hope you'll be happy. There'll be a supper-dance tomorrow night so you can meet your new friends and neighbors.' He coughed. 'Adelaide Rawtenstall, would you step forward, please?'

This was it. Taking a deep breath, Adelaide stepped forward.

'Adelaide,' the headman continued, 'on Damnation Island is a man by the name of John Maggott. His accomplishments and good deeds have made him a highly respected member of our community, and it's fair comment to say he is the most esteemed man on our island. He specifically asked for the hand of the first woman to set foot ashore. I'm told you are that woman, and you have already been designated to become his wife.. Do you agree to this?'

Pride and apprehension shivered through Adelaide. Pride at being chosen for a man with good standing, even though it was sheer luck she was the first woman ashore. Apprehension as she realized she'd have a lot to live up to. She nodded her silent agreement.

'Good.' The Headman cleared his throat again. 'John Maggott, please step forward and take your bride.'

From the middle of the line, the youngest of them all by the looks of things, stepped a young man with a shock of red hair and freckles. 'I'm John Maggott.'

Before it had time to register properly with her that this young man was her husband, another man, taller with thick dark hair, his stern expression almost a scowl stepped forward. 'I'm John Maggott.'

And one by one, all the men stepped forward, laughing now, slapping each other on the back. Behind their hands, the other women stifled giggles. Only Adelaide didn't laugh, seeing nothing remotely funny in this situation.

Even the headman was smiling. He held up his hand. 'Boys, boys, do you want your own wives to feel second best? Come now. Allow John Maggott to step forward.'

'I'm John Maggott.' Briskly, the bandy-legged man stepped forward.

Just as briskly Adelaide's heart dropped in her body like a rock in the water. Without doubt he was the ugliest man she'd ever laid eyes upon. She didn't know how she'd be able to hold a conversation with him without feeling revulsion. And as for bedding him...

He held out his hand. Her first instinct was to turn and run, but there was nowhere to go. This was the price she was paying for Daniel's safety. She had to do the best she could.

From John's ugly weather beaten face shone the kindest blue eyes she'd ever encountered. She held her breath as his gaze searched her expression, as if seeking some sort of aversion to his looks. She made sure he didn't find anything.

'Welcome home, Adelaide.' He held out his hand to her.

Adelaide offered her own hand in return. His grip was surprisingly warm and strong. Immediately she relaxed and recalled Luke's words to her. 'If we do the right thing, neither of us will miss out.'

She relaxed, and slipping an arm through his, and they walked together, heads high, towards his home.

* * * * *

In the crow's nest high above the water, looking out over Damnation Island, the wind whipped the moisture from Luke's skin, stripped the tangy sea-spray from his lips, tore the salt of unshed tears from his eyes. One last glimpse of his Adelaide, his woman. She never looked back. He couldn't have borne it if she had.

Grinding his teeth he drove his clenched fist into the wood of the rail, damning James Rawtenstall for his evil manipulations, his cruelty to Adelaide. Damning himself for not sitting down with Adelaide and talking with her about the Rawtenstall deal before everything fell to pieces, damning himself even more for being unable to persuade her to be his wife. She'd wanted to, he didn't doubt that. But her father-in-law's machinations had rendered her unable to trust anyone except herself.

As the ship upped anchor and slowly headed northwards, Luke's final view of his soul's passion was of her turning her back to the ocean, walking arm-in-arm with her proxy husband across the stony beach towards her new life. The fact that the padre had assured him no harm would befall Adelaide didn't help one bit.

The first thing he had to do when he arrived back in England was to reckon the score with James Rawtenstall. Level things out, man to man.

Then he'd return to claim Adelaide as his rightful bride. He had twelve months before the formal island wedding. Twelve months before the next boat was due on the island. It would be tight, but he'd make it.

Nothing and no one would stand in his way.

As he started towards the ratlines, a thin strip of black metal glinted in a shaft of sunlight. Curious, he bent to retrieve it. A hairpin. Several strands of long wavy hair were attached to it. He held them up in his hand. The sun's rays shone through their black warmth, tingeing them dark-blue. He didn't need to question who they belonged to —he would have known them anywhere. Adelaide. Slipping them out of the clip, he pressed them gently to his cheek, as if he would hold her one last time in his arms. Then he carefully put the clip and the stands of hair inside his shirt pocket, close to his heart, a relic of his soul's passion, and descended to the deck far below.

CHAPTER TWELVE

At the end of the windswept headland stood a single dwelling, lonely and remote. A hiding place or a hellhole? Adelaide couldn't tell for sure. But as she walked arm-in-arm with John towards her new home, Adelaide's aching heart took solace from the tug of the wind in her hair, the warmth of the sunshine upon her face. The quiet, broken only by the rhythmic plod of their feet upon the earth gave her courage. She'd never been particularly vain and didn't consider herself a beauty, though she knew she was far from unattractive. John, on the other hand, was downright ugly. But he was fit and healthy and had good friends, according to the headman's praise of him. He hadn't allowed his physical impairments to stand in the way of his life. And neither would she. It was just possible life could have dealt her a crueler hand. She'd make the best of what she had here.

A herd of cows, ever curious, followed them at a safe distance. John turned around. One cow left the rest of the herd and nuzzled John.

'I didn't think cows did that,' said Adelaide in amazement. 'I always thought they were shy creatures.'

'So they are.' John smiled grotesquely at her. 'But with patience on your part, they learn to trust you. Course, we eat them eventually, and I think they sense that, too. The thing is to be kind enough to take them away from the rest of the herd to be slaughtered. No unnecessary cruelty and things rub along smoothly. Killing is part of life here. Cruelty isn't.'

'I don't know what to say. In England I bought meat from the butcher without a thought of where it came from.'

'You don't need to think about it here either. The men do that. We look after the animals, but we don't have them as pets. That's the difference. And each household kills only what it needs to eat. No part of a beast is wasted. To do otherwise would be wicked.'

Put in those terms, Adelaide could live with that, she knew. She'd have a lot to learn, but she could adapt. She hoped.

John Maggott appeared decent. That was a good start.

They resumed their walk, John again taking her arm in his. Around a corner and out of view of other houses stood a hedge of tall pines lined with a dry-stone wall about five feet high. Just past mid-way the wall was broken by a gateway which was framed beneath an archway of old-fashioned roses.

John unlatched the gate, and it swung open. Before she could move to pass beneath the archway, John lifted her, still carrying Daniel, in his arms.

'We always carry our wives across the threshold. Makes for a fertile union,' he said.

Gently he put her down on the other side. 'I could carry you both all the way inside, but I thought you might like to look around first.'

Adelaide laughed nervously and looked about her. In front of her was a white-washed stone cottage covered by a thatched roof.

'Like it?' asked John.

'It's charming.'

She couldn't say anything else. Suddenly the journey, the loss of Luke, coming here, made her intensely weary.

Apparently sensing her fatigue, John said quietly, 'We'll go inside, and I'll make us a pot of tea. You're probably tired after your journey. We can look around the gardens later.'

He opened the door, and they went into the kitchen. From the oven came the delightful aroma of fish and vegetable stew. Flowers on the table too. The house felt welcoming. Adelaide began to feel more optimistic.

'Sit down in one of the rocking chairs,' said John. 'They're more comfortable. I'll make us a hot drink. And there's some fresh baked scones too! What about the little 'un? Will he have some tea?'

Adelaide laughed gently. 'I'm still feeding him myself. Thanks anyway.'

John filled the kettle from the tap at the stone sink and placed it on the hob. As soon as it began to whistle, he poured water into the pot and stirred it with a spoon. Two minutes later he poured the tea into china cups.

'When you've rested I'll show you around. Your luggage should be arriving shortly. No doubt everything will be strange to you for the first few weeks. Alice Miller, one of our neighbors, is to be your mentor. Her and her husband have been my lifelong friends. I think you'll like her. And there's always me, Adelaide.' He handed her a cup of tea. 'How was the sea voyage?'

'Long. We had a very rough storm. Everyone was sick except for about four of us. For days we looked after them all.'

John watched her very carefully as she spoke. The depths of her sapphire eyes looked weary, strained. And sad, though she was doing a good job of hiding the sadness. 'Have a bath and lie down,' he said kindly. 'I'll make up a crib for your baby. If he cries and I can't quieten him, I'll come and get you. I'll waken you in time for supper. What's the baby's name?'

'Daniel.'

'Daniel and I will be just fine together.' He took Daniel from her and the little boy laughed. 'I'd guess him to be around three months old?'

Adelaide was pleased at his perception, his accuracy. 'To the day.' Three months to the day since the news that Danny had been killed. It seemed a life-time ago.

John cradled the little boy in his strong arms, and a fraction of despair lifted from her soul. She'd got what she wanted —a place far away from her home town where she'd be unlikely to be found by anyone searching for her. She'd certainly got that. John Maggott seemed decent, kind even. But she was isolated from her own country and her own people —even neighbors on the island. That was something she hadn't bargained for.

John took her hand and guided her through the neat parlor to the bathroom where he turned on the taps, and the water cascaded into the old bathtub. 'There's bath crystals and skin moisturizer. They're for you. Use whatever you like. What you don't like we can give away. While the water's running I'll show you to your room.

He clasped her hand once more in his and led her down to the end of the corridor to a wooden door. 'This is the main bedroom,' he said as he opened it. In the centre of the room was a magnificent four-poster bed, the posts obviously master-carved. Before she had time to comment on its great beauty John had closed the door, leaving her alone, the only sound being that of his footsteps dimming down the corridor.

With a thick mattress and assortment of plump pillows the bed enticed Adelaide to lie down, just for a moment. Before John's footsteps had died away Adelaide was asleep.

Outside the picturesque cottage, the prettiest on the island, the rain clouds drifted purposefully across the skies, and as they crossed the air-shafts above Damnation Island, they slowly let loose their miserable load.

* * * * *

John Maggott had bought himself a handful. He'd got the things he'd wanted —a wife and the first woman ashore. With her wind-blown raven hair framing her face with its porcelain skin and rosebud mouth she was a beauty, young enough to be enchanted by all life had to offer. Her eyes troubled him. Lashes as dark as ebony, as silky as a midsummer's night, fringed sapphire globes that should have illuminated the world with their radiance. Instead, they held the look of a hunted animal, scared and desperate. It was just as well he had a spare room. He needed a wife. But not at any cost. She'd come to his bed willingly or not at all.

Before that he had to get her to trust him, so he could discover what exactly she was running from. And that could take time. John Maggott was used to giving time. It healed most things and allowed new aspects to develop.

He walked down the passageway of his house, turned the bathwater off and strode into the small bedroom. Taking a drawer from the chest he created a crib for the baby. Then he made up the spare bed for himself.

* * * * *

In his shed, John whistled as he worked. Almost finished. A canvas sling supported by a wooden-frame for his back. He put Daniel inside and tried it on for size. Perfect. He walked back to the house and began to prepare the potatoes for the evening meal. He wasn't going to be a beggar at the feast. He'd be master-carver at his own table, whatever that might entail.

There was every chance that when Adelaide had rested for a few months, got over the agonies of childbirth, the sea-voyage and whatever she was running from, she might wish to re-think her position. That would be understandable. She was a woman of great beauty, and he sensed tremendous inner strength. Why else would she go to such lengths to protect her child? For that was what she must be doing— running from something serious— he knew that as surely as he knew the grass died off in winter. With her looks, she could have got a husband in England. And when she'd regained her strength she probably wouldn't want a man who was old enough to be her father and ugly as sin into the bargain. He smiled. He'd been born ugly and used it to advantage. As a boy he'd auditioned hard for the role of Quasimodo in a school production of 'The Hunchback of Notre Dame.' He'd got the part —not just because of his looks, but because he'd put his heart and soul into it —and played the part to perfection. His parents had been appalled at the time, but with persistence he'd talked them around. And the accolades had been well worth it. The only extra prop he'd needed had been a cushion for his back. The island folk were used to his looks, and they didn't seem to mind. With Adelaide it was different. While he knew he could be a good husband, he sensed she was like a bird in a cage. Trapped. He'd be the best friend he could to her. And when he judged she was sufficiently recovered, he'd offer her her freedom with no strings attached. If she stayed with him and they got on, that would be wonderful. If she chose to leave, she could go freely, and he would have repaid some of the kindness he'd received from various people during his life-time and for one reason or another, been unable to repay.

In the meantime he'd do his best to ensure her stay on Damnation Island was a successful one. The best way he knew to do that was to keep his part of the marital bargain, care for her, be a friend and not put demands on her.

Daniel felt comfortable on his back. The little boy didn't protest, and John took that as an acceptance of him. He put the dinner-plates on the table and went to waken the woman he hoped would become the new Mrs. Maggott.

CHAPTER THIRTEEN

The supper-dance was held in the Community Hall, a medium-sized building on stilts that towered over the beach at Thunder Bay. At the base of the stilts, the surf pounded and foamed onto the rocky beach

As they walked up the steps, the hum of excited chatter from indoors buzzed in Adelaide's ears. John turned to her. 'How do you feel about tonight?'

'Nervous.'

'There's no need to be, Adelaide. These people are my friends. They are also yours. It's impossible for you to put a foot wrong, so just be yourself. Relax and have a good time. Dance with whoever you wish,' he hugged her to him, 'But save at least one for me.'

Adelaide looked at him. 'I mean it,' he said. 'This is the best way to meet your new neighbors. And let me tell you, you are by far the most beautiful woman tonight. In that green silk dress you look absolutely stunning!'

John was trying hard. She hoped she wouldn't let him down. She smiled into his eyes as he led her inside. She looked about her. The rafters were festooned with colored streamers and balloons, the walls and wooden floor of the hall were alive with music. Long trestle tables had been joined together and covered with dainty cloths. Small posies of wild flowers studded each place setting. Someone tugged at her arm. She turned around. It was Beatrice, but not the Beatrice she'd first encountered on board ship. This Beatrice, in a soft oyster-grey dress, with luminous skin and dancing eyes, looked positively radiant. Around them the air was crackling with the electricity of anticipation

'Adelaide,' she began excitedly, 'my husband lives at the top of the promontory. You know that castle-like house? That's his! It's got cellars and attics. I'm sure it must be haunted, but Peter swears it isn't. By the way, did you know your husband is the most highly thought of man on the island? Peter says everyone respects and trusts him!'

Adelaide could understand it. If he treated everyone the way he'd treated her since her arrival, she was not surprised at his popularity. She only wished she could feel as joyful as Beatrice evidently was.

Beatrice clasped Adelaide's hands in her own. 'Oh, aren't we lucky Adelaide? I was sure I'd be married to some ugly old coon, but Peter's so handsome I could die! You'll have to introduce me to your husband. After the mass wedding in twelve months' time or thereabouts, we're having a big party at our house. Oh, do say you'll come Adelaide. You were so good to me on the ship. I couldn't bear for you not to be there!'

Before Adelaide could reply the band started, and a tall man with dark features, brooding good looks and a captivating smile claimed Beatrice and led her onto the dance-floor.

Then John came and took Adelaide onto the dance-floor with such speed her breath was taken away. He was a dancer second to none, even better than Luke. She wouldn't have thought that possible, but it was. In her entire life Adelaide had never danced the polka or any of the other dances. Step-by-step John guided her through each phase of the dances with the finesse of a master. And as they moved across the dance-floor, keeping time with the music, other dancers and each other, Adelaide's spirits slowly lifted. She began to feel she'd been born to dance. It wouldn't remove Luke's mark from her soul, but it would give her something to work with. Adelaide was so delighted, she hugged him.

'Time for that later,' laughed Beatrice's husband, as they came to a stop behind them.

Adelaide danced with other partners, but John was by far the best. He made her feel, if not vital and alive, better than she had since she'd left Luke. Her energy might well re-appear, she acknowledged, and as supper was served, they sat down together.

'Enjoying it?' he asked.

'Enormously, ' she said, surprised, delighted to discover it was true.

'Good. We have these dances every week. It's one of our ways of socializing.'

'Will we come again?'

'You bet.'

'What about a baby-sitter?'

'Alice will do that for as long as we wish.'

Her feet still wanted to dance. For the first time since leaving the ship and Luke, Adelaide felt her smile reach her eyes, not just her lips.

As John took her in his arms again, talking to her, making her laugh as they danced, her hair moved around her shoulders with joy, and she felt a freedom she'd never known before. This was her new home, and these were her new people. Things might not turn out too badly after all.

She just needed to forget Luke.

John took her glass, filled it with fruit punch and took his place beside her.

'Like it?' he asked, his voice like warm honey.

'Very much.'

'Tomorrow I've something special for you.'

'Tonight's special.' Adelaide spoke truthfully, placing her hand in his. Before tomorrow they had to go home together, to bed, and Adelaide was nervous. Not the nervousness she'd experienced before losing her virginity, not the nervousness she'd felt before sharing her body and soul with Luke. This was the nervousness of knowing she had to share her body in the bed of a stranger. Without passion or physical attraction. John was a kindly man and good company. He was respected among his peers, and not once had he shown any surprise about Daniel. They could build some sort of decent relationship, and Adelaide could be a good and dutiful wife. For all his deformities, John was physically very fit. Surely he must also be virile?

Plates of desserts were being handed around when John whispered in her ear. 'Excuse me. I must leave you awhile. There's plenty of people here, and I'll be back later.'

'Where are you going?'

In reply he put his finger to his lips then hers, smiled and said, 'I have work to do' and disappeared, leaving Adelaide without a partner.

Work at a time like this? What did he mean? Adelaide had no idea. She didn't want to stay here without him, not if they were going to make a life together. She'd go with him and insist on helping. As she rose from the table, a heavy pair of male hands pushed her back down.

'John's got work to do. You're to be his wife. You'd better stay here. He'll be back soon.'

'I'm going to help.'

'You're not. You'll stay here till he's done.'

Hurt and angry, Adelaide wasn't going to be locked out of the life of her husband by anyone.

'And if I don't?' she challenged.

'If you don't, you're not worthy of him.'

She stayed where she was, as the stranger sat beside her. 'You don't know John very well yet. He never does anything without good reason.'

She'd bear that in mind and make sure she was involved in all decisions and actions in future.

Adelaide's back was to the stage when the music started again. Not a plate clattered, not a chair squeaked, all eyes were on the stage behind her as a male tenor, his voice deeply resonant, sang 'O Solo Mio' with such passion and grace she had to turn around. John! He was full of surprises! Enthralled by his singing, Adelaide turned around to face him, and when he finished, she was the first on her feet, putting her hands together to lead the applause.

When the clapping died away, she turned to the man who'd

forcibly held her down, 'Did you know he was going to sing?'

The man smiled. 'Obviously you didn't!'

This was John, her ugly, proxy husband, a kind and upright man, a good dancer with a brilliant singing voice.

Adelaide smiled. Life could have been so much worse. If only she could get over Luke.

* * * * *

They were both laughing at one of John's jokes as they opened the door into their home. Adelaide sat down at the kitchen table for a cup of cocoa. 'Why didn't you tell me you were so talented?' she asked.

John looked at her steadily. 'It's not my talent. It's a gift on loan from the Lord. It came with my good looks, and who am I to question either of them?'

Adelaide looked at him steadily. 'Who is anyone?'

John smiled. 'Drink up, it's bed-time. I'll talk to you later. Goodnight.'

He rose abruptly from the table and left the room. Adelaide shivered. Was he really a God-fearing man, or was it all bluff to hide how he felt about his looks? She didn't know. He was obviously a man of passion and talent and probably deep emotional feelings. She'd have to be careful she didn't tread on them and hurt him. He hadn't displayed any of the ill-temper of James Rawtenstall, but she wondered if it lurked in the depths of his soul. She doubted it. While he no doubt could become angry, as could anyone, she felt sure it would always be a just anger, never a malicious one.

* * * * *

The house was silent as Adelaide undressed, put on a white silk nightgown, combed her hair, put out the light, climbed into bed and waited for her husband. The four-poster bed was soft, comforting. They could have a good marriage, she knew. John had gone to a lot of trouble to make this room sensual. He couldn't be shy, so where was he?

Darkness crept into her eyes, narrowing her vision, shutting down her senses and when it ebbed away, the birds were singing outside, welcoming the first fingers of dawn as her eyelids slowly drew apart.

It was the smell of frying bacon that forced them fully open. The pillow next to hers was exactly as it had been the previous night.

She jumped out of bed, snatched her dressing-gown from its hanger, tied it at the waist and hurried into the kitchen, to find John busy at the stove.

Adelaide brushed her hair back from her face, partly in surprise, partly in apology for sleeping later than he did.

'Shouldn't I be cooking?' she asked.

'There's time for that later,' he replied kindly. 'You still need to rest after your long journey. I want you to enjoy yourself before you get into the domestic work.' He placed a large plate in front of her. Adelaide looked at it. Bacon, eggs, mushrooms. 'I hope you'll like it,' he said. 'Eat up. I've already packed lunch.' He pulled something from behind his back, 'What do you think of this?' he asked proudly. 'I made it myself.' It was the papoose for carrying Daniel.

Adelaide was stunned. 'I think you're very clever,' she smiled. 'When are we going to use it?'

'Today. Can you and Daniel be ready to leave in half an hour?'

'It's hardly daylight.'

'That's why we've got to hurry.'

He placed his hand on hers. Work-worn and sun-browned with a sprinkling of strong blond hairs on the back, his touch was both gentle and strong, with a magnetism that seemed to flow from him to her, at once demanding and reassuring. She enjoyed his touch. Without him realizing it, he gave her vitality. He'd never be Luke. But he gave her a feeling of optimism. She hoped she wouldn't let him down.

* * * * *

The grass was dew-wet as they tramped in the breeze across the open country towards the other side of the island. The child was light on his back as John pointed out the sites of historical and natural significance to the woman he hoped would become his legal wife.

'Wasn't Napoleon exiled to this part of the world?' she asked.

'Not this island. He went to Elba and later St Helena, both of them a good way north from here.'

'I read a lot about him at school. I always enjoyed history. I would have liked to teach it, but I left school early.'

Brains as well as beauty. There was some promise here. He'd have to dig further. 'You left because of the baby?'

'No. When I was fifteen. I went to work at the Mill. I always intended to go back. Then I got married.'

'What are your goals now?'

'To provide a safe and comfortable home for Daniel and any other children I may have.'

'And when they're grown?'

When they're grown. That had been too far ahead for her to contemplate. But John's careful prodding was helping her to widen her horizons, view her options. She sighed. 'That's when I'll be able to do something for myself. Either re-education or open a hotel, something like that.'

'And you think you'll be able to open a hotel on Damnation Island?'

'I don't see why not. Someplace where travelers from ships could stay. Maybe you could give them tours of the island, while I cooked. It could be good fun. What do you think?'

John remained silent a moment then said, 'I'm older than you, Adelaide. I've done a lot of what I set out to do. But it's good that you've got your sights set on the future. We can discuss them further as we get to know each other better. For the immediate future I want a good wife. Not just a housekeeper. I want a lover and companion, someone to share dreams with and plan for the future with. And children who will grow and be able to take over the homestead and keep their families well. I want them to have a good education and be able to move away from Damnation if they wish to.'

'But it's idyllic here, John. Why would they want to leave?'

'The outside world is changing. The next generation will have to be able to change with it. That's why I wanted a wife from the outside, to help any children keep up with the pace of things away from the island.'

That was logical, she knew. 'We should be well-matched.'

'We'll see. That's why we've given ourselves twelve months till the mass wedding. A sensible idea, don't you think?'

'I think it's very practical.'

Practical was the operative word, John knew. What he didn't know was how realistic it would be to have a woman as beautiful as Adelaide shut up with him on Damnation Island. The age difference was a concern, of course. But she was intelligent. And that could make them or break them. They hadn't talked much since she arrived, but today, as they got to know each other, things would be different.

'Tired yet?' he asked.

'You're joking! I love being up at this time of day, don't you?'

'It's the best part of the day for me.'

'Back home we were always up early. Evenings were for sitting and talking. And reading.'

'Did you read a lot?'

'All the time.'

John's heart lightened. 'What kind of books?'

'History, as you know. And adventure stories. Tales of explorers traveling into the heart of Africa, that kind of thing.'

'There are quite a few of those kind of books at home. Help yourself to them.'

He was surprised to see her blush. 'I already have done. I didn't think you'd mind. I've got "Travels in the Congo."'

John smiled at the beautiful woman beside him. Things were shaping up nicely.

Before them, the grass stopped abruptly. 'Do you remember a whispering as we were crossing the fields? Like the sound of the wind in the trees?" John asked.

'Yes.'

'It wasn't the wind, it was the ocean. Look, over there, the morning's still grey. You'll need to crawl the last few yards.'

They laid Daniel carefully on the grass and together dropped to their knees and crawled to the edge of the cliffs, to look down at the sand, dozens of feet below them. 'See those marks that look like tractor marks?'

'Yes.'

'What do you think they are?'

'I've no idea.'

'They're the tracks of the female turtles. They come here at night to lay their eggs. The hatchlings return to the ocean after dark. If they don't make it, they roast in the sunshine. We can come and see them make their way to the water when they've finished incubating, if you like.'

'Sounds like a version of 'If they can't stand the heat from the fryer they shouldn't be in the kitchen,' said Adelaide and shuddered.

Her shudder didn't escape his attention. 'What are you so frightened of?'

'Nothing. I was...just thinking, that's all.'

'That's good.'

She stared at him wide-eyed.

'It's good you were thinking,' said John. 'You need time to yourself. To take stock of your life. To decide if you want to stay.'

'I made up my mind about that before I left England.'

'Precisely.'

'I don't understand...'

'By all accounts you had an arduous journey here. I've heard how you looked after the sick passengers, gave them encouragement. But more than that, when you arrived your eyes were scared. They had dark rings around them. That was more than the effect of the journey.' He stopped, took a deep breath and continued. 'Whatever your past, Adelaide, work through it. Regard your first months here as a holiday. If you want to talk, I'm a good listener, and I've got broad shoulders. But think carefully before you commit to staying here. Remember your son and do whatever you think is right by him.'

'That's very kind, but what's in this arrangement for you?'

'Only this. Any marriage can only work with equal commitment. We can't live in each other's pockets. There can be no secrets. Take twelve months to think about it. In the meantime regard my home and everything in it as your own. If you decide to stay, that's wonderful. If you return, we'll both have made an extra friend.'

'I came here to be with your wife, John. What's changed your mind?'

'Adelaide,' he took both her hands in his, 'I haven't changed my mind. There's nothing I'd like more than to take you to my bed. Once I did that I'd never be able to let you go. But I hadn't reckoned on Daniel. He's a lovely child. While I'm more than happy to take him as my own, you need time to adjust to not having his natural Dad around. I'll care for you both while you're here. Just be certain you make the right decision.'

She looked up at him, her beautiful eyes misted with tears. It was all he could do to keep his hands off her. She smiled, and his soul groaned with the effort of not touching her.

'I promise. Thank you.'

'No thanks needed,' he said gruffly. 'Between friends there's no sorry either. And now it's time for us to take our little hatchling home.'

He stood up and turned in the direction of home, walking so quickly Adelaide had to almost run to keep pace with him.

CHAPTER FOURTEEN

John carried Daniel in the papoose on his back all the way home, which was just as well, Adelaide knew, as she was exhausted.

'The fresh air will have made you sleepy,' he said. 'I'll make a cup of tea while the bath's running for you. Then you can nurse Daniel while I cook dinner.'

John was worth his weight in gold, Adelaide knew. She could be content, even happy here. It had been an idyllic, enchanted day. If this continued she would never want to leave. Ever. England and James Rawtenstall's threats seemed a long way off. As did Luke. She'd never get over him, but maybe, just maybe, she could learn to live without him. There was nothing underhand or dubious about John. She could stay here. There were only a couple of matters to be cleared up.

Several days would elapse before she would have the opportunity to broach these subjects.

* * * * *

The morning sun streamed through the bedroom curtains bright and clear, trapping dust motes in its rays. Adelaide's half of the bed was warm. She stretched her hand to the other half. As usual the pillow next to hers was undented, the sheets cold. The situation needed to be talked through, resolved. But how?

The answer came as she poked her feet out of bed onto the

floor.

She dressed and walked through the airy house to the kitchen.

On the table was a small posy of flowers with a note. It read simply, 'Gone fishing. Your breakfast is in the oven. Back at dusk. John.'

That meant she'd have all day to prepare. She ate her breakfast, washed up and set to work.

As she put her hands in the back of the kitchen cupboard her fingers found an old varnished wooden box. She pulled it out and carried it across the kitchen to the table. When she opened it the light shone on an entire canteen of ornate but tarnished cutlery. She took out a spoon and turned it over. Hallmarked silver.

Working hard, polishing and rubbing each piece till the tarnish disappeared and the silver gleamed, Adelaide watched the reflected sunbeams dancing prisms of light off the kitchen walls. She hummed a tune under her breath. When the cleaning was completed, she washed her hands and fetched the tablecloth she'd embroidered on the ship, the one with the picture of Pendle Hill, laid it on the parlor table and set two places with the silver tableware. She'd like John to see where she came from. And she'd like him to see how the cloth and silverware complemented each other.

Eventually when the sun slanted light through the western trees, and the afternoon shadows grew long, and dinner was simmering, she took a bath, and standing in front of the gilded mirror in her room, brushed her black hair till it shone, pinned up the sides with red combs, allowing the dark waves to cascade over her shoulders and down her back. She chose a modest dress, —a charcoal grey one with buttons down the front for easier feeding of Daniel and a lace collar. Something was missing. She took the ruby earrings that had belonged to her mother, fitted them snugly into her earlobes and returned to the kitchen. Everything was ready.

There were matters to be cleared up between them. The first was any misunderstanding about Daniel's parentage. The second was why John hadn't visited her bed.

She appreciated he may want to get to know her properly

before consummating their union. That was admirable. However, he may well decide to send her back to England and James Rawtenstall. Under no circumstances could she allow that to happen.

Deep in thought she was carefully placing the wine glasses on the table, so didn't hear John come whistling down the path and open the door.

'My God, Adelaide.' His words made her jump. 'You're beautiful.'

Adelaide smiled and lowered her lashes.

'And when you do that, I don't know how I'm going to keep my hands off you!'

Shyly, Adelaide ran her hand through his thick hair. This was her chance. 'Maybe...'

'Don't say it. I MUST keep my hands off you if I'm to keep my promise.'

'But you've been so good to me, John!'

'And if I'm to stay good, you're going to have to have more decorum than this!'

She looked down. "I thought this dress WAS modest.'

'Of course it is...it's also full of promise.'

'Shall I change?'

'Let me revel in your beauty.' There was a slight ragged quality to his voice. 'Just for this evening.'

He filled the two crystal goblets with wine, handed one to her, closed her fingers around the stem of the glass and kissed them. Then taking the other glass, he raised it to his lips. 'Good health!'

'And an earthy life!' she laughed.

John choked. 'Christ, Adelaide, you make things difficult.'

'How old are you, John?'

'Thirty-six.'

'I'm eighteen.'

'Do you realize I'm old enough to be your father?'

'Started young, did you?'

He laughed, but didn't answer her question.

'Tea's ready. But only for those who are good.'

'I promise. I'll be very good. Don't push me too far, or you'll find out just how good.'

When the meal was cleared, they sat in armchairs on either of the hearth, talking quietly. John had been looking forward to having a wife to share his life for so long. He enjoyed Adelaide's company, and here he was with a ready-made family. It wasn't what he had expected, but he felt confident he could grow into the role. And then maybe they could have children of their own. But that was for the future. He cleared his throat.

'There's something I've made for Daniel.' He paused. 'It 's a cot to match the four-poster bed. I hope you'll like it.'

'Thank you.' Adelaide smiled her delight. 'I'm sure I will, and I'd love to see it. But first, there's something you need to know, John.'

'Go ahead.' John's tone was grave, wondering what was to come.

Adelaide's expression grew serious. 'I don't want you thinking Daniel was illegitimate. His father and I weren't married long. He was killed in the war. We got the news of Danny's death the same night Daniel was born.'

'I'm sorry,' said John, 'that must have been very hard.'

She gazed at her hands as they twisted themselves in her lap. 'Harder than you'll ever know.'

'And you had no family to help out?'

'My family died of diphtheria.' Her tone was sad.

'What about Danny's family?'

'The in-laws? They blamed me for Danny's death.'

'In the war? That's ridiculous.' John felt explosive anger on Adelaide's behalf, but was careful not to let it show.

'They had a point. You see, I was expecting Daniel when we got married. We would have married anyway. Daniel just helped things along a little, that's all.'

'On purpose?' He looked at her intently.

'Of course not. Sometimes these things just happen.'

'And what did you learn from it?'

'Not to trust in-laws?'

John smiled at her words. 'You may well have learned that

lesson if they gave you a difficult time. What else did you learn?' His eyes searched her face, met her eyes briefly. 'Tell me from your heart the overriding lesson you learnt from this drama.'

She wrung her hands in her lap, stopping when she saw he had noticed. Taking a deep breath, she met his eyes, saw in them kindness and honesty, the demand for truth, and replied, 'I learnt that I will do anything to protect my son, to keep him with me till he's grown.'

'And your in-laws stood in the way of that?' John pressed.

'My father-in-law wanted to buy Daniel from me. He saw him as a replacement for his own son. He's a ruthless man who will stop at nothing to get his way.'

John pressed his lips together thoughtfully. 'So you ran off to Damnation Island, hoping to escape his clutches, coming to a place where you imagined he'd never be able to find you?'

Adelaide felt trapped. This wasn't going the way she'd planned. The only way forward was blunt honesty. She took another deep breath and continued. 'I didn't 'run off' as you put it. It was an option that was available. I took an opportunity, that's all.'

As if sensing her unease, John said, 'I'm not trying to corner you, Adelaide. I'm just curious as to why a woman with your beauty should choose to become a proxy bride to a man she's never met.'

'I didn't see my position as running 'from' anything, rather it was running 'towards' something. Making the best of whatever opportunities presented themselves.'

'What else have you learned?'

She shrugged. 'I give up. What else?'

'That if you don't want babies there are ways to stop them getting started in the first place.'

Adelaide blushed and laughed. 'No, John, I didn't think of that one. For someone who lives on a remote island, you're very worldly wise.'

'Is that such a bad thing?' he asked gently.

'Not necessarily.'

'Tell me, Adelaide, how do you view your husband now?'

'Which one? You or Danny?'

'Both. Let's start with Danny.'

Adelaide sighed, picked up her wine glass and twirled it between her fingers for a few moments before answering, watching the wine revolve slowly, watching the cut crystal edges of the glass catching shards of light from the fire and throwing their shadows around the walls. John was forcing her to look deeper into herself than she was comfortable with. She had no choice but to continue what she had already started.

'I loved him very much. We'd made great plans together. He was tender and kind.' She recalled the sudden smile that lit up his face whenever they met, like a warm balmy breeze on a hot summer's afternoon. 'It seems a long time ago, now.'

John smiled. 'You've been very frank, Adelaide, thank you. Danny was your husband, your first love. You bore his child. He'll always be part of you. Treasure his memory; it will make the grieving easier. You need to remember that's why I don't come to your bed at night. I want to give you time and space. That's all. Let's move onto something else,' he said, and pulled out the chess-table and put it in the space between them.

Adelaide smiled as she made the first move of the game. She wouldn't have admitted it, but she felt relieved. The air was clear.

She hadn't told him about Luke. There was no need to, was there?

CHAPTER FIFTEEN

John hefted the heavy axe to his shoulder and brought it whistling past his ears to land with a satisfying crack in the centre of the old pine log, splitting it into two. As he worked into a fast rhythm, he began to relax. He loved the vigorous, tangy smell of the gumwood as it dried out in the sunshine in preparation for the winter fires. He had someone to provide for, and life was even better than it had been previously. Especially now that the air was clear between him and Adelaide. He hoped things would stay this way. After several minutes he stood back, wiped the sweat from his forehead with the back of his hand and would have started again were it not for the crushing pain in his chest. He leaned into the long handle of his axe, allowing it to pass. It wasn't as bad as the last time he'd had an attack of indigestion, but he'd take things a bit easy today. Perhaps it was a pulled muscle? If it continued over the next week or so he'd see the doctor. Maybe. In the meantime he'd enough firewood for the first couple of months of winter.

As the pain began to ebb, John stacked the split logs against the lean-to to dry. He entered his workshop and put away the axe. Then he walked across the wood floor to his workbench, reached his hand up to a hook. He took down some sandpaper in one hand and one of the planed pieces of wood from his project in the others. He enjoyed sanding, and he sanded it till it was as smooth and as even as a woman's thigh.

This was one part of life he really enjoyed, taking something plain and transforming it into something beautiful or useful. Not much longer now, then he could present it to Adelaide. He hoped she'd be pleased with it. A hammering in his gut was telling him to prepare for every contingency, that there was little time, to make sure that everything that needed to be done was done. His instincts led him well when he was hunting. There was no reason not to follow them now. The same gut feeling also warned him that he was going to be very busy in the months to come. But that was common sense, wasn't it? He wiped the wood clean of the sanding dust, replaced it with the other parts of his project and went inside to eat.

* * * * *

Early morning sunrise flowed rapidly and smoothly into the warm golden glow of sunset, and as the days passed quickly, the easy companionship between Adelaide and John deepened. Their relationship was much different to the one she had shared with Luke. Different, but still good. Whenever she put her hand to her throat and accidentally touched the emerald pendant or caught a passing glimpse of the magnificent gem in a mirror she was reminded of Luke. Luke. Every night he was in her dreams. Would he ever come back to her? She wanted to think so, but he didn't have long before the island wedding —a matter of just under a year. Experience had shown her the answer would be no. Despite all his protestations that he'd loved her as she'd loved him and would always love him, she didn't think he'd come back. She'd told him she couldn't trust him ever again. She'd said she didn't want to see him again. It would be easier for her that way. Expect nothing and you won't be disappointed. Every morning she awoke expecting to see his face at the window. It was never there. The fact was she'd lost everyone critical to her happiness —her family, Danny and now Luke. Her in-laws had turned against her. Not that they'd ever liked her. She had no reason to trust anyone, least of all, Luke. The only people she could trust were those under her nose — Daniel and John Maggott.

Other than that she kept too busy, learning how to cook to

John's taste or helping in the fields, to grieve overly for the love she and Luke had shared. Daniel grew plump and rosy-cheeked, while Adelaide's skin acquired the lightest of tans, the beautiful pale bronze peculiar to those with the fairest of all Celtic complexions.

And she enjoyed her time with John. He proved such a witty and interesting companion; her mind was enthralled by him. On the lonely island there was little news from the outside world, therefore Adelaide grew to look forward to the evening meal with John, when they'd discuss the running of the island, various aspects of agriculture and possible foreign trade.

After the meal they'd retire to the nook where John would read to Daniel, even though he was too young to understand. But the little boy would laugh and smile as if understanding John's intentions. Adelaide loved these times. She loved even more the time when Daniel was asleep, and John would read poetry with such passion in his voice, she couldn't help but be seduced by his mind.

If she'd never known Luke she could have been content, maybe after a while happy, with John.

CHAPTER SIXTEEN

The horse's hooves gently cupped the soft earth beneath them as Adelaide sat astride the big animal. John held her in front of him, one arm encircling her waist, holding the reins in the other. It had been a fun evening in the big house on Thunder Bay. Beatrice and Peter were fine hosts. They'd played the piano and sung, and after a superb meal cooked by Beatrice and served by Peter, they'd played cards. Roast wild boar with cranberries, laughter with friends and now the comfort of John's strong body behind her as they made their way home. The more time she spent with him, she more she enjoyed his company. She had a pot of gold at the end of a shimmering rainbow. Riding bareback was fun, and John tightened his arm around her as he nudged the horse into a gentle canter. The moonlight slanted shadows from the trees in their path. Deep in the wood an owl hooted and was answered by her mate. A rabbit hopped quickly across the track in front of them to scurry and hide in the undergrowth.

Seeing how quickly Beatrice had settled into her new life, Adelaide realized how easily she too was settling. It wasn't only John's kindness that helped. He had a strong personality and was good fun.

She was looking forward to the next day when she'd ride over alone and help Beatrice organize a bottom drawer of baby-clothes for the large family she hoped to have. With the gentle breeze in her face and John's strong, comfortable body behind her, Adelaide felt safe. She had a husband. Beatrice and her husband-to-be were like extended family, and Adelaide was a fortunate woman.

When they arrived home, John lifted her from their mount and brushed his lips briefly, tenderly across her hairline. Then he shut the horse in a field for the night, and they made their way to the cottage.

Pushing open the door to their homestead, John said softly, 'Close your eyes, I have something for you.'

She sat down and closed her eyes, opening them when she heard a light thud on the table. In front of her was a wrapped parcel.

'It's for Daniel' he said, 'but for you to open.' Gently she undid the wrappings, and allowed the paper to fall away. What she saw took her breath away.

In front of her, carved from gumwood, was a replica steam engine complete with whistle, large painted wheels, chips of gravel glued on to the tender to resemble coal and carriages attached to it by short chains.

'I know you must be homesick. Just thought it'd be nice for the little 'un. That's all.'

'I hardly know what to say!'

'Say you'll be my wife. Tell me we can have children together.'

'I'm already proxy married to you.'

'You know what I mean.'

Adelaide didn't reply but stood up and threw her arms around him and kissed him tenderly on the mouth.

He felt different to what she'd anticipated. Unyieldingly sinewy, with the warm, musky smell of male permeating them both. His kiss was pressing, urgent, as his arms tightened around her waist, and he drew her close, running his fingers down her back, to the flare of her hips. He felt good, but as his breathing labored she wasn't ready. She needed more time. John didn't hurry. Gently he kissed her, held her, stroked her. Over and over, loving her, as if they had all the time in the world. His kiss was tender, caressing, and when her lips parted, he breathed into her, and Adelaide's body began to respond to his. A slow, measured response, born of friendship and deep affection. As her lips parted further, his tongue met hers, exploring the recesses of her mouth. His arms encircled her, cradling her in his embrace, protecting her. She felt safe, valued, as one would value the most exquisite piece of porcelain. His kiss deepened, and Adelaide's body stirred with his. As her breasts peaked, gently he ran a strong hand down her back, warm, comforting and capable, to her hips. Her arms wound themselves around his strong shoulders, down his muscled back, to his hard, firm thighs. She opened her mouth further to explore his, as he found the front of her hips, the soft curve of her belly, upwards till his hands brushed, then cupped the swell of her breasts. Gently, with great control, he waited for her arousal to match his. She leaned into his embrace, her breasts pushing into his strong chest, wanting him to touch them, kindle them into life.

With a shaking hand he pulled the pins from her hair, and it cascaded over her shoulders, her breasts. Tenderly he unfastened the buttons of her bodice and put his head down to kiss the rise of her softness. She stroked his head, urging him on, as her needs began to keep pace with his. Slowly, tenderly, he worked his way down, kissing, teasing, till his tongue laved her rosy nipples, now hardened and firm. From underneath them, his hands lifted each breast to his mouth, as he took each one in turn. Her legs suddenly weak, she leaned back against the wall, whether for support or in some pagan form of submission, she neither knew nor cared. Her breath came in soft gasps as his body, hard and demanding, leaned into her belly.

As a soft moan escaped her lips, John swung her into his arms and carried her quickly to the bedroom, placed her on the magnificent four-poster bed and firmly closed the door.

* * * * *

As the moon outside rose higher, drawing out myriad unknown and unremarked stars, spreading them throughout the velvet carpet of night, John loved Adelaide, gently, tenderly, bringing her to crest after crest of pleasure, allowing her to rest there awhile, never allowing her over the top.

And as night hitched up her lacy skirts and began her long trek from the skies, John introduced his enormous manhood to her entrance. A sigh, deep and soulful, rose unbidden to her lips as Adelaide moved to accept him. He moved in a slow rhythm, hard and deep, and when the rising sun chased away the last remnants of night, John was still driving into Adelaide, a hard, comfortable rhythm, a rhythm that promised safety, security, permanence. A rhythm that promised physical passion, acceptance and friendship, and who knows, maybe that would even lead to love?

When it was finally over, John slept. Beside him, physically satisfied and emotionally hopeful, Adelaide rested, heedless of the single tear that slid down her cheek as Luke's face was the last thing her mind saw before she too, fell into a relaxed slumber.

CHAPTER SEVENTEEN

A bellbird sang joyfully in the gumwood tree outside the window, the tinkling notes piercing Adelaide's sleep. The happy tones filled her head, ran down her spine, to the pit of her stomach.

Adelaide opened her eyes, took a deep breath and gently swung her feet to the floor. The first wave of nausea struck. Seconds later she was racing for the bathroom.

As her stomach muscles contracted a stream of vomit shot from her mouth, splashing into the porcelain toilet bowl. Her legs turned to jelly as spasm after spasm of sickness wracked her body.

As suddenly as it had started, it was over. Adelaide rinsed cold water onto her face, showered, surprised herself by feeling ready to face the day and went to find John.

'Breakfast's ready,' he said, placing bacon, eggs, tomatoes, mushrooms and fried bread in front of her.

Adelaide didn't want to be a nuisance. She ate what was put in front of her. All of it. And again had to race for the bathroom. John followed her, holding her as she once again emptied her stomach contents into the cold porcelain bowl.

'Here's a cloth for your forehead,' said John, wiping her face. 'I think you should stay in bed for the rest of the day. I'll take care of Daniel.'

'Thank you. I'll be OK. It's probably something I ate last night.'

'Maybe,' said John. 'But I'm not unwell. Let's wait and see, shall we?'

The following morning the sickness was totally incapacitating, lasting throughout the day. Adelaide was unable even to move her head without retching.

* * * * *

Each night Adelaide thought the next day she would be better. Each morning she was a little worse. Every night John slept on the bedroom floor, in case he was needed during the night.

For three weeks the sickness persisted. The mornings were appallingly bad, with the sickness abating towards the end of the day. In the evenings when she was feeling better, John would gently lift her from the bed and carry her to an armchair by the parlor fire. Then he'd hand Daniel to her and read them both a story from a book taken from the inglenook.

* * * * *

Beatrice and Peter had been to visit after Church, as had other friends. Presents were left, in the form of flowers, books, home-made jams. It was a Sunday evening, and the first day that Adelaide hadn't been sick.

When the visitors had left, John helped Adelaide to walk into the parlor. The weeks of not eating had taken their toll, leaving her feeling as weak as a kitten.

Daniel was in his cot, and John and Adelaide were sitting by the fire, watching the flames race up the chimney, when John spoke softly,

'Tell me the truth, Adelaide, are you pregnant?'

Startled, she replied, 'Of course not.' Then, 'How could I be?'

'Your sickness gets better at night. You've lost weight. Your hair shines more than usual. And you've gained girth around your middle.'

'John, we've had one night together. Wonderful as it was, I wouldn't have started getting sick the next morning. Would I?'

John didn't answer, merely handed her a cup of beef tea. 'That doesn't answer my question. I won't ask you again.'

*****

That night, John and Luke chased each other restlessly through Adelaide's dreams. As they raced, Danny came to join them, smiling. She awoke with a start. My God! She'd been sick with Daniel, but nothing like this. How long had she been on Damnation Island? Almost three months now. She'd never been regular, but she was way, way overdue. Gently she pressed a hand to her tummy, just below the navel. Sure enough, there was a hard little knot! Oh no!

She'd have to talk with John. But how and what to tell him she had no idea. To make things worse, she'd more or less denied any possibility of being pregnant.

When she rose from the bed and walked into the kitchen, she found it empty. On the table was a note,

'Not sure when I'll be back. There's wood for the fire in the brass box by the hearth. If that runs out, open the seats in the inglenook, and you'll find plenty more there. I've brought a ham inside for you —it should last till I get back. The veggies are in the garden. J.'

John had gone. He'd known she was pregnant, recognizing the signs before she did. And when she hadn't admitted it, he'd withdrawn, she knew that. He was a good man, and he deserved better treatment than this. He'd offered her the safety of his home, cared for Daniel as if he were his own child, shared his land, his friends, his hearthside and his soul. He hadn't condemned her like James Rawtenstall had done. He'd even gone so far as to tell her to take her time with her decision about staying here. If only she'd been more aware at the time, more sensitive to HIS needs. If only she'd told him about Luke. She'd been frank about Danny, anxious that John knew that Daniel wasn't illegitimate. Anxious that John knew she hadn't spread her favors willy-nilly among the male population of Lancashire. Anxious that he should think well of her. She hadn't told him about Luke, and now it was too late. This was shabby repayment for his kindness.

And yet...there was a spark of joy. She ran her fingers down the swell of her abdomen. Luke lived inside her. A thrill of pleasure shocked through her. She was carrying Luke's child. He said he'd come back for her...but would he? More to the point, would she want him if he did? Her soul screamed yes. Her mind warned her that he had worked for James Rawtenstall. She loved him, but couldn't trust him. She trusted John, but couldn't love him. Not in the way she'd loved Luke. Or Danny. What a mess!

It was as she stood at the kitchen sink washing the dishes, with the sunlight flowing in a golden stream through the window that Luke's words came back to her. 'Do what's right, and everything will work out.' Adelaide didn't know which way things would work out, but she knew she had to do the right thing. And that would be to tell John about Luke when he returned. If he wanted to hear. If he didn't want to hear, she'd be on the next boat back to England. And James Rawtenstall. She heaved a deep sigh. Until recently she HAD always done what was right, but she couldn't honestly say her life was any the easier for it.

The days were long, the nights lonely, and Adelaide's tummy began to swell. She missed his company, his ready wit and his story-telling.

* * * * *

High above his head the bellbirds sang in the gumwood trees, as John Maggott ascended the rocky mountain track to his usual camping place. Normally the birdsong soothed him, making him feel at one with nature. Today the noise irritated him. He swung his knapsack from his back and placed it in the undergrowth at his feet. He told himself he'd come here to hunt. The real reason he was here was to think. Adelaide was pregnant —he'd stake his life on that. But he couldn't think in his own home. Adelaide needed a safe haven; he'd no doubt about that. So he'd left her in the home that had been passed to him through generations of his family. In peace and comfort. He himself had 'gone bush' for awhile.

There was no doubt in his mind that he loved her, not merely her physical beauty, it was her inner beauty that appealed to him.

But what about the father of the second child? Surely he had a right to know Adelaide was carrying his child. He couldn't understand why she wasn't with him. Her morals were certainly not loose. He'd have known if they were.

He strode through the clearing, gathering twigs to start a fire upon which to cook a meal. His choices were limited. He loved her. He could insist they marry straight away, for the baby's sake. Or he could give her time to think. Sending her back to England was not an option.

He'd give her all the time she needed and hope she would formally marry him. He could no longer conceive of a life without her beauty, her goodness and her laughter.

* * * * *

One morning, unexpectedly, Adelaide woke to the smell of frying bacon. She jumped out of bed, dressed quickly, combed her hair which now fell way below her shoulders. Then she went into the kitchen and threw her arms around his neck.

'John, I thought you'd never come back!'

'You didn't really think I'd leave you here alone, did you?' He was surprised, but pleased at her reception of him. Had she missed him after all?

'Well...'

'I've been hunting, that's all. We've enough meat for a year now.'

'We have to talk, John.'

'You're right. We both know it's serious talk, don't we?'

'Yes.'

'We'll talk tonight over dinner. Put on your prettiest dress. We'll make an occasion of it. Don't look so worried, Adelaide. Look.' He took hold of her hands. 'We both know what we've got to talk about. Let's not make a drama of it. I'm older than you, and nothing fazes me. I've got work to do now. Wear something pretty for tonight.'

* * * * *

Adelaide chose one of her looser dresses to conceal her burgeoning figure, an emerald green one that matched the pendant she wore around her neck. The one from Luke.

John had said not to make a drama of it. Things might yet turn out all right. Not well, but at least acceptable. On the other hand she could well find herself on the next ship back to England. She couldn't blame John for that, she had to admit. Perspiration beaded her upper lip as she dressed. It pooled under her arms. She was afraid. Not of John, never afraid of dear, kind, gentle John. She was afraid of the mess she was in. Reluctantly she had to admit, this one was of her own making. Unwittingly she'd dragged John into it. What she wanted, needed to do, most of all was to put her head on her arms and weep. But tears didn't come easily to her. Besides, they wouldn't solve anything.

She gritted her teeth and dressed her hair into raven ringlets that cascaded with abandon down her shoulders to her back.

* * * * *

A fire roared in the hearth, casting shadows of warmth and hope on the parlor walls. In the centre of the table stood a candelabra holding three lighted candles. A long-stemmed red rose lay by Adelaide's place-setting.

Silently, John served the meal she'd prepared. It was John's favourite —wild goat and roast vegetables.

Neither of them ate much, and both were silent. She'd have to talk sooner or later, she knew. She didn't want to hurt him any more than was necessary, but she knew she'd hurt him all the more by NOT speaking.

Finally, mustering all her courage in both hands, she said, 'John we need to talk.'

'Let's not spoil this dinner, shall we? You're a good cook, you know?'

'And you're a good man, John.'

'You're not a bad woman, Adelaide. Don't forget that.'

'Who goes first, you or me?'

John hesitated, then said, 'I will. I'm sorry to have left you alone for several days. It was inexcusable in your cond...with you being new here and a nursing mum. I know you've been very honest with me, Adelaide. And I think I've been honest with you. But the fact remains that there are things in both of our pasts that may be painful to talk about.'

A flush, hot and shameful, rose to Adelaide's neck. She lowered her eyes, unable to meet his.

'I've listened to you talk about Danny, how Daniel was on the way when you married. And I think I've told you to treasure your memories. In an ideal world, we wouldn't have any secrets from each other, would we? Not if we hope to marry and make it work.'

The flush became hotter, rose higher to her cheeks. 'No, but...'

'No buts, Adelaide. You see, I too, have something in my past that caused me tremendous sorrow. That's where I've been the past couple of days. I've come to terms with it now, I think. At least as much as I'm ever going to. But I don't want to talk about it. Ever.'

'That's fine, John.'

'Good. There's nothing between us, then, is there?'

'Er...there might be...that is to say...'

John took her hands and led her to the seat by the fire. 'You can't tell me, can you?'

She shook her head, miserable in her desolation.

'What would be worse —telling or not telling?'

Adelaide stifled a sob.

'OK not telling would be far worse, wouldn't it?'

She nodded her head.

'Look into the flames and tell me.'

Adelaide took a deep breath.

'John, I'm sorry, but I'm pregnant.'

'Didn't I say that a few weeks ago?'

'Yes. I'm really, really sorry. I had no idea. I'll take Daniel and go back to England on the next boat.'

'You're in no condition to travel.' he remarked mildly. 'Besides I enjoy having you around. But tell me about the child's father —did you love him?'

'Very much.' As baldly as that. She couldn't believe she'd said it. Then she told him about Luke, how she'd discovered he worked for James Rawtenstall, how betrayed she'd felt. How she felt she'd betrayed John. The tears flowed freely, tears she hadn't shed since she'd discovered Luke's betrayal. Everything came pouring out.

'That necklace padlocked around your neck, that's from Luke, isn't it?'

She nodded. 'Cut it off.'

John shook his head. 'No. It looks to me like a very valuable piece of jewelry. And it's yours. He wanted you to have it. Enjoy it. It's part of your history. It's what makes you the wonderful person you are today.'

When Adelaide had finished crying, John held her in his arms and dried her tears.

'We've known enough of each other to say we're friends, haven't we?'

Adelaide nodded.

John continued. 'Here's what I suggest. Don't have your baby out of wedlock, Adelaide. It's not fair on him.' He thought hard before continuing. 'We'll bring the wedding forward, have it privately in this house. That'll stop tongues from wagging. I'll look after you during the birth and afterwards.' He'd delivered cows and sheep by the hundreds over the years. A baby could well be different, but if they ran into trouble there were plenty of people they could call on for assistance.

'That's very kind of you, John,' sobbed Adelaide, 'but I can't put you through all that.'

John ran his hands across her hair, stroking it gently. 'It's no trouble, Adelaide.' He didn't want to lose her now. He would be having a larger family than he had anticipated. But he would do what was best for her, even if that meant losing her. 'The boat calls once a year, unless there's an emergency — that gives you just under nine months to think. Take that time to think what you want to do about your future. And Daniel's. And the new one. If you then wish to return to England so be it, and I'll pay all your fares. You know I'd be happy to have you stay here as my wife. But there's something else you must know. Since you've been here, I've had the happiest times of my life. If and when Luke returns, you may go to him if you wish. I won't hold you to anything you don't want. Is that a deal?'

Adelaide thought hard. She had thought Luke to be the love of her life. And he was. But John was a good man, and she was very fortunate to have him by her side. She'd also grown to love him in a way she'd never known would be possible.

'You're a good man, John. I don't deserve this. I've come to love you, too. In a different way to Luke, different again from Danny. But it's there. It's different, but no less valuable for that. I just wanted you to know.' She hesitated. 'I also want to do what's right by you.'

'Thank you. You need to rest now and rest your baby. You've had a sad and difficult time. No decisions are easy. None of us is perfect. We just do the best we can.'

He bent and kissed her forehead tenderly, patted her on the shoulder and took the dinner plates into the kitchen.

CHAPTER EIGHTEEN

Luke Collins was pleased to have his feet once more on solid Lancashire ground. Every step he took was taking him nearer his Adelaide and their future together. All that lay in front of him was a confrontation with James Rawtenstall. While it would surely be tricky, it wouldn't be impossible. The steel caps of his heeled boots clipped the flagstones, echoing loudly as he walked along the deserted, rain-swept street towards his destination. He was a man with a mission. The first step was to find James Rawtenstall and preferably around town rather than at his own home or in one of the Mills. On neutral territory. That way they'd meet as equals, talk man-to-man.

It didn't take long. He pushed through the door of 'The Queen's Head', the smell of beer and stale cigarette smoke searing his nostrils, honing his senses. Through the layers of smoke, his eyes searched the crowded room, as he strode casually to the bar counter before anyone could notice a stranger. Before there could be a lull in the conversation. It wouldn't do to be too obtrusive. Not now. He walked to the bar, ordered a pint of Thwaites beer and turned around, his back against the hard counter, his eyes scanning the other patrons.

In various dimly-lit nooks sat an assortment of drinkers —most of them couples. He drained his glass and made his way into the saloon. Here, the air was thicker. Conversation was quieter, punctuated occasionally by the hollow echo of a billiard cue hitting a ball, the gentle whoosh as that ball rolled across the green felt into a pocket. An atmosphere of intense concentration surrounded the table. On the far side was James Rawtenstall, cue in hand, shirt sleeves rolled up. 'Come on,' he was saying to his opponent. 'Lose this and you lose your home.'

The conversation dropped to a whispered hush, and an uneasy silence fell around the table.

Rawtenstall's opponent was a young lad, barely sixteen, by the looks of things.

James Rawtenstall hadn't changed in his absence.

The young lad was shaking as he took his shot. And missed.

'Send someone to tell your parents to start packing their furniture,' Rawtenstall snarled to the lad.

Luke strode to the table, and when it was the lad's turn again, a murmur of anticipation arose from the spectators. Silently he took the cue from the lad, took aim, pocketed the ball and won the game. A round of applause echoed cheerfully throughout the saloon.

James Rawtenstall looked up slowly, his features grimaced into a scowl.

'Step in where you're not needed, would yer?' he demanded.

'Seems to me I stepped in exactly where I WAS needed!' said Luke. Then, 'Now this young lad can safely keep a roof over his head, why don't I buy you a drink?'

'I'll have a whiskey-all-in. Double.' Rawtenstall snarled.

Luke nodded to the barman, speaking politely. 'You heard the gentleman. We'll have it over here, please.'

He addressed himself to Rawtenstall. 'Right, cock. Let's get down to business. Your grandchild's safe.'

'What...? I thought I recognized you,' Rawtenstall muttered through a cloud of alcohol breath. 'Where's the mother?'

'They're both on Augustus Island.'

'I paid you to bring 'em back yer smart-mouthed bugger!'

'You paid me to find out where they were. You haven't paid me anything yet to bring them back.'

James Rawtenstall clenched his fists. 'Yer wouldn't be thinking of getting smart with me, would yer, lad?' snarled Rawtenstall.

'Just stating a fact.' Luke said evenly.

'So where is she?'

'They're both safe.' replied Luke evenly.

'Safe from what?'

'You, for a start.'

'Eh?' he said drunkenly.

'Sober up, then I'll talk to you about bringing them back safely. The mother's afraid of you, Rawtenstall, as are most people around here. If you want her and your grandson back you need to forgive her for marrying your son. She could come back here, lead a decent life, and you could see your grandson,' Luke said reasonably.

Without warning, James Rawtenstall turned, upending the table as he did so. 'Not bloody likely! She's killed my son, and there's no forgiveness.' His hands caught Luke by the throat, and he squeezed. Luke put his own hands, thumbs inwards, onto Rawtenstall's wrists and eased his attacker off.

'Wrong!' said Luke quietly. 'You're a bully, Rawtenstall. This time you've met your match!'

Rawtenstall balled his fist, swung a hard punch at Luke. Luke ducked, and the punch missed.

'Your family'll be the next out of a house. I'll have them evicted tomorrow!' James Rawtenstall yelled.

Luke didn't recall thinking or even feeling anger. All he recalled later was the cracking grind as his knuckles connected with Rawtenstall's nose, the blood splaying over the walls. Before Rawtenstall had time to fall down, Luke moved in one fluid motion, picked him up, slung him over his shoulder like an old sack of potatoes and carried the mill owner out into the night.

Outside 'The Queen's Head' the night air was crisp and clear. Above them, stars studded the black carpet of night. Rawtenstall lay heavy across Luke's shoulders, almost a dead weight. But not quite. He groaned as Luke turned a corner leading to a dark alley. When he was sure he had not been followed, Luke bent forward, sliding Rawtenstall's weight from his shoulders. Before the older man could sink to his knees Luke grabbed him by the lapels of his coat, forcing him back against the cold red bricks that made up the wall of the backyard of the pub.

'Let's reckon things up for a moment, shall we?' he said. 'Adelaide married your son.' He hit James Rawtenstall, not hard enough to knock him out, just hard enough to keep him aware.

'Your son loved Adelaide. She loved him.' A thump to the chest.

'Your son went to war and was killed in action.' A thump to the abdomen. Rawtenstall doubled over, coughing.

'I'm going to marry Adelaide, and we're going to live here safely and happily.' Two slaps to the cheek, each one making Rawtenstall's head turn as red welts arose. Another thump to the abdomen.

'You're going to figure out a way to come to terms with that.'

'Never!' James Rawtenstall spat blood and teeth into his hands. He staggered up and pulling a baton from inside his coat, swung it over his head, aiming at Luke.

Luke's hand shot out, and he caught it in mid-flight. Rawtenstall fled down the alley. Luke smiled to himself. At the end of the alleyway, Rawtenstall slowed down and turned around. 'She's knocked-up, second-hand goods. Always has been. Always will be. That's what you're getting yourself into. Just like my poor boy did...my poor, poor boy...'

Luke's fingers curled around the smooth wood of the baton, tightened, and he hurled it in Rawtenstall's direction. It whistled through the cold night air, missing Rawtenstall's ears by millimeters as it knocked down the collar of his coat on its forward journey to land with a hollow thump on the cobblestones.

'Next time you won't be so lucky, Rawtenstall. Pick up your baton, go home and look after your wife. She'll be no doubt grieving for her son. God knows how she manages to put up with you.'

Luke dusted himself down and watched the broken figure of James Rawtenstall shamble out of the alley.

* * * * *

Luke Collins had been walking the streets all night. He'd lost his temper. What that would cost in the long-term he'd no idea. But cost it would. Few people tangled with James Rawtenstall. Fewer still got away with it. But he had no regrets. Come hell or high water he was bringing Adelaide back to England. And he'd ensure her safety. One way or another.

His finely honed senses picked something in the early morning air...smoke...far off, but even from here smelling bad. Following his nose, he raced along the darkened pavements, passing through the amber glow of the street lights, into the darkness again. He rounded a corner, almost tripped on a night cat out tomming. He straightened and turned into Pemberton Way. At the end of the street was Bank Top Mill. One of Rawtenstall's holdings. Smoke belched from the back of the building, the smell acrid, stinging his nostrils. The street was deserted. Was he the only one aware of this?

Gasping he finally arrived outside the mill. It was shut up. He climbed up the stone wall to peer inside. Smoke swirled densely behind the window.

He retraced his steps, searching for a public phone box. There was one on the other side of the street. He raced across the cobbles, pulled the heavy red door open, picked up the receiver, dialed 999. 'Bank Top Mill's on fire,' he said.

'Is anyone inside?' asked the voice on the other end.

He didn't know. The voice assured him the fire engines would be dispatched immediately. Luke put down the receiver and started again in the direction of the mill. It was Saturday night. The night-watchman would be the only person there. Where was that man now? It could be twenty minutes or more before the fire-engines arrived. He'd have to go in and check himself.

Inside the windows, smoke was swirling around the glass. He didn't have much time. If someone was trapped, he needed to go in now. He circled the building. All the doors were locked. He put his shoulder to the night door, pushed and almost fell inside. A paroxysm of coughing hit him as the smoke scorched a path into his lungs. In the distance he could hear the eerie wail of the fire sirens, quickly coming closer. Next to a bale of smoldering cotton lay the body of the night-watchman. Luke bent down. The man reeked of whiskey. He felt for a pulse. Weak and rapid, but better than nothing.

As Luke dragged the inert body into the fresh air, to safety, a heavy hand fell upon his shoulder,

'You're under arrest, sir!'

*****

James Rawtenstall shut his front door loudly. He didn't have the strength left to slam it. His damn fool wife, Margaret, appeared from nowhere with a cup of cocoa. He knocked it from her hands and sank bonelessly into an armchair. His head ached; his entire body ached from his fight. He looked down. His clothes would never be the same again. But he had his revenge, making Collins pay for what he'd done. He'd phoned the police after the fire incident, disguising his voice, telling them he had seen Collins start the fire at Bank Top Mill. In a low voice he told Margaret what had occurred. Margaret made no comment. She was used to his vindictive ways.

'Put your head back,' she said finally, with her usual saintly patience when he'd finished speaking. He couldn't be bothered to resist, as she dabbed at his cuts with a cloth and soapy water. Bit by bit he felt comforted. When it was done, she emptied the water into the sink and disappeared.

Whenever he came home drunk she'd always undressed him and put him to bed. Why not now, for God's sake? He didn't have the energy to call her back. He'd sleep in the chair. That'd teach her.

He looked drunkenly around the room. Everything he'd built up for his son. The bikes, the trout fishing, the house on The Hill. The best education for Danny. The Mills. He'd put his son before Margaret, who'd never questioned, never complained. How had she felt? How did she feel now? With a start he realized this was a question he hadn't asked himself for years.

Was it too late?

It was too late for him and Danny. But him and Margaret? Surely she still cared. This was the first time he'd been beaten in years...where was she?

He dragged himself sluggishly out of the chair, and went upstairs to their bedroom. The door was shut. He knocked softly.

When there was no reply he knocked louder and tried the handle. Locked. He shook the handle, whispering as softly as his drunken state would allow. 'Margaret – it's me.'

On the other side of the door was silence. Rawtenstall put his shoulder to the door and pushed hard, once, twice and heard the wood splinter. He pushed again, the lock gave way, and the door groaned open. Margaret stood in the centre of the room, arms folded. In the middle of the bed lay a suitcase, half-packed. His anger gave way to bewilderment. 'What's going on?'

'I'm leaving.'

Rawtenstall laughed nastily. 'Leaving? Nobody leaves James Rawtenstall.'

'Adelaide did. And she took Daniel with her.'

'Yer've nowhere to go.'

'That's where you're wrong, James.'

'Wrong?' His voice rose. 'I'm never wrong!'

Margaret kept her voice even. 'I've cleaned you up for the last time.'

Ratwenstall balled his fist.

Margaret took a step towards him. 'Touch me with so much as a hair from your body, and I'll press charges against you so heavily you'll be salami on the market stalls!'

Rawtenstall shook his head drunkenly. 'What's got into yer, lass? All your life you've been a quiet little mouse.' His face cleared. 'Oh, I get it, yer've got yerself a fella, some fancy pant dandy no doubt, waiting for you.' He nodded his head. 'All these years and I thought, really thought that I had you and Danny to meself.'

'Stop feeling so sorry for yourself, James,' Margaret snapped at him. 'Yes, I'm leaving, but not with a fancy-man. If you hadn't been so tied up in seeking revenge on Adelaide you would have known.'

'Known what? Are you sick?'

'Sick of you, that's all. When my father died he left me a house on Todmorden Road – the one you said would never amount to anything. From the day Danny got married, I've watched jealousy eat away at you. You couldn't even give Adelaide the time of day. When Adelaide finally left – and I couldn't blame her for that – I had the house converted into small flats.'

From outside came the sound of a group of people singing as they walked along the street. 'Yes, James,' she said softly, 'that's the sound of normal people enjoying themselves.' She paused. 'I know what happened at the pub last night. I know about Luke Collins, how he saved the night watchman from certain death and how you had him thrown into jail. You never even considered that Luke Collins could have been a good substitute son for us. That's why I'm leaving you. I love Daniel and Adelaide and they love me, and I'm inviting them and Luke to join me in Todmorden Road.'

Rawtenstall blanched.

'That way I'll have the family I love around me, and you'll have no one so think about that. You've never loved them, James. You treated Daniel like a possession, that's all. If you make things difficult for us, I'll refuse you any access to them. And that's my final word.' She finished packing her suitcase, buckled the straps and dragged it across the floor to the door.

'Margaret, stop, please. I'm begging you.'

Margaret hesitated and turned to face her husband. 'Why? You've never cared for me. The only one you've ever cared for is yourself and your Mills.'

James Rawtenstall fell upon his knees and crawled across the floor to Margaret, where he flung his arms around her knees. 'Don't go,' he sobbed. 'I can't manage without yer. Isn't it enough that I've lost Danny?'

'WE lost Danny. He was my son too, don't forget.'

'All these years I've taken yer for granted. Eh, I'm sorry lass. It's just that you've always been so reliable, and now I can see what I've driven yer to. Tell me please, what do I need to do to make yer stay?'

Margaret took his arms from around her knees, 'Let's go downstairs and have a cup of tea. Then I'll tell you exactly what you need to do to make me stay and to straighten things out with Adelaide, Daniel and Luke.'

CHAPTER NINETEEN

On the morning of the wedding Adelaide drew back the pink curtains, secured them to the sides of the window with ribbons and gazed out. A thick veil of mist had rolled in from the sea, cloaking the island in a shroud of white silence. Not a bird sang, not a tree groaned. The only sound that reached her ears was the slow lap-lapping of the ocean as it brushed the sand below the cliff.

This was her wedding day. The day she'd pledge herself to John, forsaking all others, promising to cleave herself only to him. And not before time, she thought, stroking the bump around her abdomen. If only it were John's, she wouldn't feel so bad. Could she really go through with it, knowing that if Luke turned up after today, to claim her as he'd promised, she would be unable to go to him? Her heart still yearned for him, would always yearn for him. Just as her heart, indeed her entire psyche resisted hurting John. Dear, kind John. Never in her entire life had she encountered another human being with such a degree of kindness, of compassion. What if she were to back out now? John trusted her. He had shown her time and again that he would never hurt her. Or Daniel. He'd provided and would continue to provide a safe haven for them away from James Rawtenstall's clutches. There was no logical reason not to go ahead with the wedding.

Adelaide was so engrossed in her thoughts she didn't hear the gentle tap on the bedroom door. Nor was she looking when the door opened, and a slender figure slipped into the room.

'The bride looks out of the window on her last day of innocence!'

Adelaide turned round with a start. 'Beatrice!'

'John said I could come in and help you get ready. He's a lovely man, one of the best. It's going to be a beautiful day for you both. Oh, Adelaide, I wish you so much happiness.'

'Thank you.' She smiled. She couldn't tell Beatrice she was carrying Luke's baby. That would be an unfair burden on everyone, —herself, John, Beatrice and Luke. Luke. Did he have any idea? Did he care? She shrugged. He was far away, and for the moment that was what counted.

She bathed, dressed her hair, made up her face. Beatrice took her to one of the spare bedrooms and said, 'Close your eyes. Your wedding dress is in here. John says I have to put it on you, but you can't see it till after the wedding.'

Beatrice helped her into the dress, and Adelaide reveled in the silken touch of her gown as it cascaded in folds to her ankles. Side by side they walked to the parlor. Adelaide reached the doorway and stood stock-still. Dozens of vases of lilies decorated the table, the bookshelves and every available flat surface. The air was heady with their fragrant perfume. But it was John who took her breath away as he greeted her.

Always fastidious about his personal hygiene, he looked almost handsome in his morning suit.

A beautiful setting and John. This was so typical of his kindness. It was going to be a lovely day, after all. If only she could get Luke out of her mind!

She heard the murmur of the minister's words, heard John take her for better or for worse, in sickness and in health to his lawful wife. Suddenly she was being asked by the minister to forsake all others till death them did part. A picture of Luke rose unbidden before her. Take John and forsake all others. That meant Luke. Her baby needed a father. She knew John would fulfill that role beyond all expectations.

A soft moan escaped her lips. A lump rose to her throat. She swallowed hard, hesitated and said, 'I do.'

Taking her left hand in his, John placed a plain gold band upon her finger, and Adelaide became Mrs. Maggott.

'Adelaide,' he said, 'you are as fresh as the dawn, as beautiful as the sunrise, as serene as the dusk when the sun sleeps at the end of the day. Turn around and let our guests see how lovely my wife is.'

Adelaide hadn't heard anyone enter the room. She turned round, astonished to find the parlor was packed with smiling friends and neighbors, every one of them dressed up in their best attire, every one of them with a flute of champagne in their hands. As one they raised their glasses.

'To John and Adelaide.'

Arthur Glass, the Headman stepped forward. 'And now, I propose a toast. As we all know, John has always wanted a family. He's already got one with Adelaide and Daniel. Here's to your beautiful bride, John. May your union be happy and fertile.' He winked at Adelaide. 'The more children you can give him, Adelaide, the happier he'll be.'

Adelaide smiled. If only they knew. And they would soon enough, there was no question of that. She splayed her fingers, looking down at the wedding band. It fit comfortably. She felt secure. A sense of contentment, wellbeing suffused her body and her spirit.

Despite everything, despite all her qualms and fears it was going to be a good day and a good marriage. John would see to that. And she would do the best she could to be a good wife for as long as she could.

* * * * *

The sun was an orange ball of fire, sinking rapidly, but gently towards the horizon, as John and Adelaide's wedding guests began to leave. One by one they assembled outside the homestead, linked around and hummed a lullaby, a tune so sweet, so moving, that Adelaide's eyes misted with tears. She was very fortunate to be here with such a good husband and wonderful friends.

'Mrs. Maggott,' he said, 'one more surprise.' Taking a silk scarf from his pocket, he gently tied it around her eyes. 'Can you see?'

'No.'

Tenderly he took her hand in his strong one and gently led her into the bedroom. 'Stay still and open your eyes.'

He removed the blindfold, and Adelaide saw them both in the full-length mirror. The wedding dress he'd had made for her was cream satin, falling in voluminous folds from a semi-fitted bodice, emphasizing her chest, concealing her growing abdomen. It was more stunning than she'd ever dreamed of. Around her neck hung the emerald pendant given to her by Luke. She should find some way to take it off, now that she was married, but she couldn't bring herself to broach the subject with John again. Later, maybe.

John stood next to her, his arm cradling the small of her back. The light from the bedside lamps lent his eyes a look of smoldering, dark passion. Behind them, the bed was scattered with rose-petals. She reached up and took his hand.

'Like it?' he asked.

'It's... it's beautiful.' Her eyes filled with unshed tears at his kindness. She blinked them away rapidly. 'Thank you, John. I hope I can live up to your expectations.'

'You will, my lovely, you will.' He turned her around to face him, dipped his head and kissed her gently, a kiss full of love and tenderness. 'You deserve the best, Adelaide. I'm going to see that you get it. For all of our life together, you will lack nothing that is in my power to provide.'

The rest of their lives together. For better or for worse. This was it. She was married to John now. Not Luke. There was no hope for her and Luke now, even though she was carrying his child.

Her gaze slid again to the bed. All this trouble. Just for her. She loved him for that. For this sort of romantic, simple kindness. For the making of the papoose for Daniel. For the making of the model train. For the small things he'd done for her son, demonstrating his kindness, his caring. And for the greater understanding of his love, his gentle acceptance of her as she was, for his non-judgmental understanding of this current pregnancy. She also loved him for his wit and conversation. His stories for her and Daniel. But the love of a bride for her husband? She couldn't love him the way she loved Luke. But she liked him, and she respected him. She could show her consideration by never letting him know just how important Luke was to her. She could improve her mind and be a suitable companion for him. She could be emotionally loyal and physically faithful. Maybe they could be blessed with children of their own. And, she promised herself, at some point in the future, when John needed her, she'd be there for him, as he'd been there for her.

She stood still as John's shaking hands undid her wedding gown and helped her step out of it, allowing it to fall to the floor.

'Adelaide, we've made love. One passionate night. We were both needy. This time I want to take our time, feast my eyes upon your loveliness. I want to enjoy you with my eyes, pleasure your body with mine, like it's never been pleasured before, feel your sweet breath upon my skin, love you till you'll love no other but me. I want to hear you call my name at the height of your pleasure. As the years go by we'll know each other's needs so well, no one will be able to take our places. I want you to remember this day and tonight as a turning point, critical to your happiness, both now and in the future.'

'John, I don't know what to say.'

'Don't say anything. There's no need.'

As he undid her chemise, the satin rubbed against her skin, teasing the rosy buds beneath.

He took them in turn in his mouth, caressing them with his tongue till they hardened. He knelt before her, his hands caressing her hips, his lips teasing the dark curls beneath the flimsy silk. Adelaide was helpless beneath his gentle ministrations. A groan escaped her lips, and her legs parted slightly as John's lips and hands worked her as if by magic. His hands rose to the flare of her hips, pulled aside the wispy silk garment, and his strong arms lifted her and carried her to the bed strewn with rose-petals. Gently he laid her against the cushions, his hands spreading her hair, as his lips brushed her hair-line, eyelids, cheeks, ear-lobes, lips and the hollows of her neck. She reached for him, his maleness.

'Not yet, beauty.' He took both her hands in his, held them on the cushions behind her. 'This time it's only when you are truly ready.'

He swiftly undid his shirt, letting it hang loose, revealing a washboard stomach, covered with dark masculine hairs that arrowed downwards. Adelaide buried her head into his chest, found his small male nipples, biting them gently. Her leg wound around his, urging him closer. She needed him. Her eyes feasted upon his strong chest, the enormous bulge of his manhood tenting his trousers. Quickly he shrugged out of his shirt, slowly he undid his trousers, and Adelaide gasped. He was bigger than any man had a right to be! Her hips raised to meet his. He lowered himself, gently, teasing, till her breath came in soft pants.

His strong hands flipped her over, his great member teasing, cajoling, as he massaged her shoulders, her arms, her back, her thighs, calves and finally her feet. Steadily he refused to give her the release she needed. He turned her onto her back and drew her up to face him, his swollen member as hard as granite against the softness of her nether regions. Her secret place that needed him most. His hands ploughed through her hair, he kissed her passionately, deeply, his breath stealing her soul. His tongue laved her ear-lobes, the indented jewel of her tummy, downwards, to moisten her most secret place. She reached down, and her hand closed around his giant, throbbing manhood to guide him into her. She felt him shudder as he bore into her, his breathing labored as he pushed every last inch inside.

'Open your eyes and look at me,' he commanded as he thrust farther, his hands stroking the backs of her thighs as he raised them across his shoulders. The weight of his great testicles massaged her inner thighs as he drove into her, his panting, heavy breathing music to her ears, in a rhythm to match her own heartbeat. Time after time John brought her to the crest of pleasure, without allowing her over the top. Loving kisses and passionate words covered her hair, skin, nails, every bodily orifice, every inch of her. And Adelaide loved in return, exploring John as a mountaineer explores an unknown mountain.

As the sun made its first appearance through the purple skies,

John allowed Adelaide her first release. From somewhere deep within her, she heard his name, soft at first, then louder and louder as he skillfully brought her to the first of their mutual orgasms.

Her legs were still shaking when John started work again. They didn't hear the cock crow outside, they didn't hear the dawn chorus of the birds in the trees. They were unaware of the cows that needed milking. The only thing that mattered was each other, their mutual pleasure and their mutual fulfillment.

As the dark fingers of dusk clawed their way across the horizon of their first full day as Mr. and Mrs. Maggott, John and Adelaide finally fell asleep, happy with their bargain and satisfied with each other.

CHAPTER TWENTY

The morning after his defeat at the hands of Luke Collins, James Rawtenstall sat at the breakfast table, the morning paper spread in front of him. From the kitchen came the sizzle of bacon, the smell of eggs and tomatoes frying. He was a fortunate man, he realized that now.

His wife of many years, a handsome woman by anyone's reckoning, thick hair brushed and dressed into a bun, brought in a plate of breakfast for each of them.

'Eh, lass, it's just like when we were first married, isn't it?'

'He was my son, too.'

'I know, I know. I just don't see how I'm ever going to be able to make it up to you.'

'The past can't be replayed, James. We're both grieving. So is Adelaide. Don't forget that. You drove her away. We'll always grieve for Danny. But we can move forward.'

'Together?' he asked, more anxious suddenly at the realization of what he'd almost lost.

'Certainly. But we do have a grandson. He's our flesh and blood. And his mother needs to be able to come home. You know that, don't you?'

'It's me pride.'

'Of course it is. You just need to put it aside, that's all.'

'Do you know what you're asking, woman?'

'Haven't I put mine aside for years?'

James Rawtenstall grunted into his breakfast.

'Eh, lass, I'd be lost without you. You know that, don't you?'

'I'm not going anywhere, James.' She smiled softly, the softness born of a difficult life with a handsome, but harsh and insensitive man, the softness that comes when once more a tiny particle of the world is at your feet.

'Neither am I, lass. Not without you. Never again.'

'Promise?'

'On my standing as a Mill Owner.'

'You know what you have to do, don't you?'

He put his hand on hers. A hand hard enough and strong enough to crack a pile of roof tiles. It was a rare gesture of respect, warmth and newly found optimism. 'With you by my side, how could I forget? I'll find young Collins this morning.'

'And?'

'O.K. I'll do as you say. I'll tell him he can bring the wench home.'

'Wench, James?'

'O.K. I'll tell him Adelaide and Daniel can come home. He can marry her and live in peace.'

'Daniel?'

'You drive a hard bargain, lass.'

'Daniel?'

'O.K. No more threats to take him away.'

'And?'

'And what?'

'What about Daniel's education?'

'I can't offer money, Margaret. It'll seem like I'm trying to buy them back.'

'Daniel is your grandson. You can let them know he'll inherit when we die.'

'Is that wise?'

'It's the proper thing to do.'

CHAPTER TWENTY-ONE

Life on Damnation Island proved sweet. As each day progressed, John and Adelaide grew to enjoy each other more and more. The days were an intellectual journey to discover each other's minds and what was in them. The nights were for pleasuring and exploring each other's bodies. While John's love-making lacked Luke's abandonment, he more than made up for that with expertise and finesse. They learned each other's wants and desires, and truly, John had turned love-making into an art form. So much so, that at times Adelaide was sure she'd felt the earth move beneath them. She didn't talk about it with John, lest he think her emotional or even worse, stupid!

The days passed into happy weeks. In the evenings, John would read for Daniel, and Adelaide sat in a chair on the opposite side of the hearth, knitting cardigans and bootees to go into the layette for the new arrival that they were both looking forward to.

* * * * *

One Sunday night Adelaide and John had attended the evening Church Service with their friends. They'd spent an hour singing hymns to the heavens, praising the Lord. Adelaide remembered to thank the Lord with all her heart for the blessings He had given her.

Later, outside the small chapel, they'd conversed with friends and neighbors then John had taken her hand, placed it in the crook of his elbow and arm-in-arm they'd walked home, to sit by the fireside in the parlor. As John was reading a story to her from one of his books, Adelaide knitted and listened, when she suddenly felt the house move beneath her, causing the plates and glasses in the cupboards to rock and the windows to rattle in their frames.

She rested her knitting on her lap and turning to John said, 'You felt that, didn't you?'

'Yes.'

'I'd thought they were in my imagination.'

'It's not your imagination, Adelaide.' John coughed and cleared his throat. 'There's something you must know. Damnation Island is volcanic. These shakes have been going on for some time. They're being monitored by seismographs in neighboring countries. As far as we can tell there's no immediate danger, and they will probably die down. But just in case they don't, we need to be prepared.'

'For what?'

'Evacuation. It probably won't happen. But any papers, treasures that you value, keep them handy.'

Evacuation. That was all she needed. If they had to evacuate let it be anywhere, but please Lord, not to England. England where James Rawtenstall would be waiting to take Daniel from her. England where Luke was. Damnation Island was her home now. She'd grown to love the place, as she'd grown to love John. He'd never be Luke. But she'd made her life with him, and she had become protective of their life together. It wasn't the same love she'd shared with Luke or even with Danny. It was different but was nevertheless very precious to her, as was John. He loved his home and his life, and she in turn, valued and respected his hopes and dreams. She couldn't prevent an evacuation. But she could do her best to ensure that if they had to leave, she could help him settle wherever they landed.

'I've got you. I've got Daniel. The babe's safely in here.' She patted her heavy tummy. 'That's all I need, John.'

John reached across to her, took hold of her hand, lifted it to his lips and kissed it. 'I hope that's enough for you, Adelaide.'

'Of course, it is.' But it couldn't be, could it? It was Luke's baby she was carrying. It was Luke who should have been here with her, sharing the joys of up-coming parenthood. Sharing their mutual love. A love she would never be able to share with John, no matter how fond she was of him. That was the difference. She had grown fond of John, and they shared a bed. The passion she had with Luke, she couldn't feel for John or anyone else. No one would ever be able to fill Luke's boots. That saddened her. She would always miss Luke, her once-in-a-lifetime love. Every time she gazed at the new baby, she would see Luke, smell him, hear him, taste him on her lips. And John Maggott deserved better than that. Why couldn't she love him as she'd loved Luke?

* * * * *

Fresh spring conceded to the balmy southern summer, not as hot as the tropics, but every bit as beautiful. From dawn to dusk cicadas whirred and chirped, and Adelaide's belly grew full and cumbersome. Christmas was still some weeks away when Adelaide started a late spring-clean, clearing unwanted rubbish from the house, so they could progress unencumbered into the New Year.

It would also make things easier in case they had to evacuate, although that possibility no longer held the same dread for her. She started with the linen cupboard, working swiftly, sorting items into various piles, sheets that needed turning, blankets and pillowslips. She had almost emptied the cupboard when her attention was caught by a hook on the back wall. Something on a hanger that was covered by a sheet. Gently she lifted it from its hook, removed the sheet, brought it into the light, and gasped. Oil paintings! Quickly she took them into the bedroom she shared with John and placed them on the floor in front of the windows to better see them in the light.

What lay before her took her breath away.

The paintings told a story. Whether true or imaginary, she had no idea. The raw, naked talent in them made her heart leap. The first picture was a woman bending to take bread from an oven. Her face was invisible, but it was the kitchen in this house! The next one showed the woman outside in a yard full of hens. She was wiping a child's face. Then came a painting of a Christmas dinner in the parlor with a dozen or so people seated around the table. How happy they all looked! The next paintings were darker, both in color and in mood. One showed three boats full of men rowing out on a stormy sea. The following one was a graveyard scene, showing women weeping by the headstones. The final one, a boy on his own, shoulders down, head bowed, standing by an open grave.

Only John could have painted them. But why would he hide them? Modesty? He'd never told her he could paint. They were good, her instinct told her. Talent like this shouldn't be hidden. And if they were indeed evacuated, this could be the key to their future. She knew now what she would give him for Christmas.

CHAPTER TWENTY-TWO

Adelaide and John awoke to hear the bellbirds singing a greeting outside their window, heralding in the season of joy and festivity, on their first Christmas morning together. The previous evening they'd cut the top off one of the gumwood trees, brought it inside, decorated it and placed presents for Daniel around the base. What a difference it was from the northern Christmas, where snow fell, where the ground was slippery and treacherous with shot-ice. Here on Damnation the temperature was warm and balmy. Adelaide sipped the cup of tea John had brought to her in bed.

'Happy Christmas, Adelaide.' Next to her teacup was a small present wrapped in gold foil. Carefully Adelaide opened it. Inside was a gold bracelet with three charms.

'I had my mother's gold jewelry remodeled for you, so you could have something just for you.'

He took the charms. 'A mill chimney to remind you of your northern roots, a volcano to remind you of Damnation Island and a stork for the baby you're carrying.'

'Thank you, John. They're lovely.' She reached underneath the bed and brought out the first of several parcels. 'I too, have something for you.'

She watched excitedly as John opened the parcel so carefully wrapped. But her excitement turned to concern as she saw the color drain from his face.

'Where did you find this?' he asked flatly.

'In the linen cupboard.' Adelaide wondered what on earth was wrong. 'I thought they'd be lovely on the parlor walls.'

One by one John silently unwrapped the paintings, a thin blue line outlining his lips.

Finally he turned to her, his tone firm, his expression grim. 'Adelaide, you probably meant well. Heaven forbid it should ever be otherwise. Under no circumstances are these paintings ever to be on public display.'

Adelaide was perplexed, anxious to know what she had done wrong. This had been her loving gift and for some reason it had backfired. John turned to her, his face a mask of anguish.

'Understand this. These paintings are private, you hear? PRIVATE! I won't insult you by taking them from their frames. No doubt you thought the idea was a good one.'

'John, you've gone grey. Please tell me what I've done!'

'Adelaide, I had a father and brothers. You've seen them in the paintings. We were a very happy family. I was the youngest —five years younger than the youngest of my brothers. They went fishing with other men from the island. The weather had been filthy for weeks, but still they went.' John took a deep breath. 'They never came back. Any of them. Women were left widowed, families were without fathers. That's what the paintings are about. Our happy family before they went to sea. The desolation when we realized they weren't coming back. These paintings are personal. Not to be shared with the world. When I'm dead, sell them by all means, but not, I beg you, not while I'm alive!'

Adelaide was devastated. The last thing she had intended to do was to hurt his feelings.

'John, I'm so sorry. I had no idea about your losses. Neither you nor anyone else had ever told me. But I'm not talking about sharing your sorrow. I'm talking about sharing your talent. These paintings are good. Don't you realize that?'

'I tell you what, Adelaide,' he said. 'I appreciate your thoughts. Why don't you let me paint a picture of you as you are now, heavy with child and positively glowing. We could hang it in the parlor. And if you really think it's good, you can send some paintings to

London to be valued.'

'I'd love that John. If we went to London together, I could take you north, show you where I come from, the moors, the mists...' If only there was a way for her to be out of the danger of Rawtenstall's clutches.

That evening, after dinner, when Daniel was safely tucked into bed, Adelaide sat in the parlor. In front of her, behind his easel John started the preliminary strokes of his painting of Adelaide. As he worked, they chatted comfortably, discussing the trip they'd take when the baby was old enough. Thoughts of evacuation they'd lived with for so long drew far away.

How could they have known their days together were numbered?

CHAPTER TWENTY-THREE

Luke sat on the bunk in his cell, knees apart, elbows on knees, head in hands. At this rate, he'd miss the next boat to Damnation Island. He'd been incarcerated here two days already.

Two days of listening to the clanking of cell doors opening and closing, meals on tin plates, no exercise. For what? No other reason than rescuing a drunken night-watchman from a blazing factory.

He got up and paced the cell floor, stopping only when he heard the metallic clink of a key being turned in the lock of the cell door. James Rawtenstall walked in followed by...this couldn't be his wife, surely? The whole town knew how badly he treated his wife. And everybody else. What the hell could they want here?

'Mind if I sit down, lad?'

Luke stayed where he was. 'Be my guest.' You'll do what you like anyhow. Always have done. You're not going to stop now, are you? he thought. Luke walked to the far side of the cell, distancing himself from their madness.

'I ...er...I couldn't come before, not till I'd got things straightened out, like. The missus here, it was her idea. Apparently you want to marry me...our...daughter-in-law.'

'Go on.'

'I knew yer were inside. But I couldn't get yer released before. Not till I'd got everything straight. It was Margaret here that helped me see the error of my ways. The night I got a beating from you. Anyway, lad I'll not go into details.' He handed Luke an envelope.

'This letter is from my solicitor, so it's all legal and above board. I want yer to take it to Adelaide. I'm giving her High Castle Craggs, a country estate I purchased some years ago. My lad Danny, well, he can't have it now. So it passes to her. I want her to have it now, not when I'm dead. Then yer can all have some peace and a bit of income. You see, when we had that fight, it made me realize what a fool I'd been. And I've almost lost my grandson into the bargain. Say yer'll take it lad, please. Don't make me beg. If it weren't for you, I'd've lost Margaret, here, too. She's a good woman, and Adelaide'll be good for you.'

'I don't know what to say...'

'Say nowt, lad. Take this letter. Your ship leaves in one hour.'

CHAPTER TWENTY-FOUR

The last leaves of summer had turned from green to red then gold. Hay had been cut, crops sown, and the swallows were flocking and taking large preparatory swings across Thunder Bay.

As Adelaide filled her lungs with the morning freshness that was in the air, the fresh tang of autumn, amiably sweeping through the house, brushed before it the last remnants of summer from all corners of every room.

She got out of bed and stretched. Today she felt magnificent. Not the slightest trace of nausea. Just a tremendous feeling of wellbeing and vitality. She lowered her hands and stroked her belly, smiling when the child inside her moved. Just once. She was looking forward to his arrival. Somehow she knew she was carrying a boy, and now Daniel was weaned she longed to suckle another baby.

Luke should have been with her. Luke. Not John. The father of her child. The love of her life. Luke. Good man that John was, she could never give him the love he deserved. The all-out once-in-a-lifetime, one hundred percent commitment given freely with both body and soul. She could be a good friend and as loyal as was possible in the circumstances. But John deserved better.

If she returned to England she'd have to face James Rawtenstall. And what about John? Technically it left him free to find someone whose love would be based on affection and friendship and would be freely given. Maybe that would be better for him than her affection which was based upon desperation and need. Technically.

But she knew he loved her and Daniel and was basing his life upon a family now, not just a couple. Was she prepared to hurt him by throwing all his kindness back in his face and leaving? Or would she hurt him more in the long-run by staying and never being able to love him as she loved Luke, never being able to forget Luke, seeing Luke in her mind's eye every time she looked at the new baby?

Distractedly she ran a hand through her hair. What a mess! The more she searched for a solution, the more deeply embroiled she became.

The infant inside her moved again, a gentle nudge this time, causing Adelaide's breasts to tingle. Not a kick or a somersault, a mindful reminder of her position. She'd have to do what was right for all concerned, not just herself. Didn't she always?

She swallowed and took a deep breath. She'd enjoy the day.

* * * * *

By lunchtime Adelaide was feeling pleased with her morning's endeavors.

Stone-fruit had been bottled, onions pickled and bread baked, and they stood on the kitchen workbench like soldiers lined up for duty. All the curtains had been taken down, washed and re-hung. The windows had been polished till they shone, the wooden floors swept and oiled. She was just about to start on a large pile of ironing when the door opened and John walked in. He looked around him at her morning's handiwork. 'Bed,' he said.

'You're joking. It's not yet lunchtime.'

He took her hand, led her into the bathroom and ran a bath. 'You're starting early, that's all.'

'Nonsense. The baby's not due for another month yet.'

'Trust me. You're glowing,' he said, pouring perfumed oil into the water and helping her into it, where his strong fingers set about a gentle massage of her neck, shoulders and back.

'How's that?'

'Glorious.' And it was. But she would have given anything to have had Luke massaging her in preparation for the birth of their child. She needed him now, more than ever. And she mustn't let it show. Suddenly the prospect of giving birth and trying not to shout anything untoward became daunting. She hoped she wouldn't let John down.

'Come to bed now.'

* * * * *

As John was helping her towards the bed, the first of her pains ripped through her body, catching her breath in her throat, rendering her unable to speak. At the same time the house shook around them, rattling the windows in their frames, causing the floor shift slightly. She had time to reach out and put her arm around one of the bedposts, but that was all. Both the pain and the shaking took an eternity to pass, and when they eventually subsided she needed the bathroom. Quickly. She turned and waddled down the passageway as best she could, but not quickly enough. As she turned through the bathroom doorway water coursed down her legs to pool at her feet. She tried to stop it, but her efforts were in vain.

John brought her a fresh night-gown and slipped it over her head. It was then that she realized the reason why she'd handled the loss of Luke so well. A part of her had known, on a purely instinctual level, that he lived inside her. She'd thought he'd come back for her. She'd really believed that. She'd taken his word. She'd always imagined he'd arrive one day, like a knight in shining armor, and take her into his arms, slip a ring on her finger, and together, they'd ride into the sunset with Daniel. She started to shake so violently even her teeth chattered.

'Your waters have broken, that's all.' He hesitated a moment, then asked, ' Is this different from last time, Adelaide?'

'Yes.' Last time she'd gone to term. She hadn't been frightened. This time she was afraid. Afraid of the stillness and the silence outside. Afraid of the smell of sulphur —like rotten eggs —that accompanied the shakes of the island. This time her labor was premature. She was afraid of losing the baby, of losing little Luke. She'd gone almost eight months. She couldn't bear for anything to go wrong now. She couldn't tell John any of this.

John helped her into bed, propped her up on pillows and began to read to her. Every hour, on the hour, he brought her a drink of beef tea. But as daylight became purple-gold in the corners of the sky, John grew concerned. Six hours had elapsed since her waters had broken, and there were no signs of further contractions.

CHAPTER TWENTY-FIVE

Luke had lost count of the number of days he'd been at sea. He put his hand into his shirt pocket and brought out the lock of hair, Adelaide's hair, and held it to his lips. It still held her perfume. He knew that every sunset brought him nearer to the woman of his dreams, his soul's mate, his Adelaide.

He'd been proud of his achievements until he met her. Then he knew as surely as he knew that the rain fell from the skies that without her, he was only half a person.

On board ship he'd spent long hours debating with himself over what would happen if she stayed with the man she was proxy married to. He'd tried to shrug those thoughts away. Adelaide had loved him. He'd seen that in her actions, her eyes, her soul. And he'd seen her devastation when she'd discovered he had worked for James Rawtenstall. Seen the fear, the distrust in her eyes. Seen the haunted look in them when faced with the desolation of Damnation Island. Witnessed the glimmer of hope, the tiniest smidgen of trust in them when he'd told her he'd be back for her. He'd seen all this, even though she herself had denied it.

It was this love that spurred him on now. He'd started off as a passenger then became a paid crew member when one of the sailors had gone down with appendicitis. And even if he'd been mistaken, if she no longer loved him, he loved her. Would always love her. Was determined to have her.

CHAPTER TWENTY-SIX

The fireplace in the bedroom hadn't been used since John was a boy, but now he was thankful he'd checked the chimney every year, clearing it of birds' nests and other debris. He strode outside and returned with an armful of kindling, put a match to it and added a couple of logs. Within minutes the room was basking in a warm, dusky glow. Outside the windows framed with pretty lace curtains Adelaide had sewn with such diligence —dark was rising. Something wasn't quite right, he knew that. It wasn't just the shakes that rattled his cottage or the surf that pounded the beach below with unusual ferocity. It was more than that. Adelaide's pains were taking a long time to get started. It was hours since her waters had broken, and still her labor hadn't started properly.

He took the torch from its hook in the kitchen and ran down the garden path, out onto the headland. The smell of sulphur in the air was nauseating. Far in the distance a light shone in one of the upper rooms of the house at Thunder Bay. He prayed he'd be in luck as he flashed his torch three times. And made the sign of the cross when he received three quick flashes in return. He flashed again, received an answer and turned for home, dropping something from his pocket into a pool of rainwater at his feet. He glanced down. Only a plastic comb. It could be rinsed when he got home. He put his hand into the puddle to retrieve it. And stopped. The water was warm, warmer than body temperature. He shook the comb dry, put it into a back pocket and set out for home, making a quick detour via the beach, where he knelt down. With his hands he rapidly pulled the wet sand aside till he reached water. Again, it was far warmer than usual, almost hot. Thoughtfully he turned for home.

Peter lived on the other side of Thunder Bay. It shouldn't take him long to arrive. He was an old and trusted friend. Not that either of them had thought his presence would be necessary. Most women on the island gave birth easily, probably due to the vast amount of physical work that was an essential part of their daily lives. But if Adelaide ran into trouble, and she might well, John needed someone on hand to go for help while he stayed with her.

Before he entered the back door he cut a large armful of lavender to put on the fire in the bedroom and some chamomile to make his wife a herbal drink. The two herbs should react well and give her some rest for what lay ahead.

The house was silent as he opened the door. He crept into the bedroom where Adelaide lay against the pillows, her eyes closed, her cheeks and forehead a flushed pink, to match her lips. She was as beautiful as Snow White must have been. He laid the lavender on the hearth and returned to the kitchen to prepare the chamomile brew for when she awakened.

Thankfully Daniel was asleep on the settee where John had left him. A quick check of the list of all the things needed —cot, sheets, boiling water and a towel. He lifted an armchair and carried it quietly into the bedroom to wait till she awoke.

As he sat by the fire in the bedroom, John mentally checked everything was in order for the evacuation. It would come now, as surely as the grass grew in spring. His soul told him that. The only question was when. He knew the headman had radioed for assistance and that assistance was on the way. The question was, whether Adelaide would manage the delivery before the evacuation or not. He'd prepared the horse and trap for a rapid move when the siren came. In the meantime, it was best she didn't know how imminent their departure was.

He must have dozed off for a while, but suddenly he felt, rather than heard her stir, and moving to the bedside took her hand in his. She smiled at him vaguely. His gaze sharpened. Adelaide's eyes were dilated.

'Would you like a drink of chamomile tea?'

She didn't answer, just squeezed his hand gently, then suddenly her gentle touch became a vice-like grip as she closed her eyes again. He moved the bedclothes down and put a hand on her abdomen. It was rock-hard. Suddenly there was a discreet plop from her treasured place, and blood, crimson as embers from the hearth and almost as hot, dripped slowly from beneath her thighs onto the white sheets below.

'It's starting, dearest,' he said. 'I'm with you and everything is going just fine.' He hoped it was, and that in a few hours from now he wouldn't be eating his words.

Taking hold of her just beneath her armpits, he pulled her up into an almost sitting position and placed several pillows behind her for extra comfort. Then drawing up her knees, each one in turn, he placed a sheet over her tummy for modesty. He'd seen plenty of cows and sheep through the birthing process, but this was a first for him. He watched her eyes close as another spasm gripped her. The pains were about thirty seconds apart, an unusual way to start, he thought. He hoped all would be well. He looked at her face. Instead of the fatigue he'd expected was an expression of intense excitement. Her eyes were laughing, her lips shining. His wife was carnally radiant. Her excitement spread to him. As she labored, he lowered his head between her thighs to better assist the birth. Suddenly the baby's head crowned.

'The baby's got black hair.' He exclaimed as the contractions closed then re-opened 'Push Adelaide, push hard.'

The tiny bundle propelled itself out, straight into John's hands, and he heard Adelaide laugh. He lifted the red bundle. 'We've got a boy!' John wiped the infant's face with a cloth, wrapped him in a shawl and handed him to Adelaide. 'Keep him at your breast. We've just to wait for the placenta.'

'Our John Junior!' Oh God, make him ours, she thought. Luke's not here. The baby needs a father. Please let John step into his shoes. Then we can have a good life.

'No, Adelaide, call him Luke. Then he can be proud of his

natural Dad too!'

John was right. He should be Luke. And Adelaide needed Luke. Right now. She held the little boy in her arms. Ten fingers and ten toes. Perfect. Like his Dad.

John watched Adelaide as he waited for the placenta, but it failed to appear. Where was Peter? Surely he wouldn't be long now? He would have to do the best he could. He palpated her abdomen, watching her face as he did so. Complications now were the last things they needed. But he'd see it through to the end. They both would.

'One final contraction, Adelaide. Push!' he encouraged.

He watched her carefully, waiting. The blood that had previously dripped from her thighs was now flowing freely. Where on earth was Peter?'

Adelaide started to pant. Again he bent his head to see what was happening. 'Push, Adelaide. Hard.'

He put his hands out to catch the placenta. Like a bullet from a gun it shot into his hands. He looked at the bloody mess and went dizzy. It wasn't the placenta at all. It was another baby. Carefully he wiped the infant's face. He was smaller than the first one, but just as perfect. He handed him to Adelaide.

'Well done! It's twins.' But before she could take hold of him, another spasm wracked her body.

John put his hands beneath Adelaide and caught the placenta. It was large, far larger than he would have thought was usual.

'One placenta, Adelaide. The boys are going to be identical!'

'This one's called John. John Junior!'

With shaking hands, John cut the cords of both babies and gave the second baby to Adelaide. She took the tiny infant. There wasn't much she could say to John, except, 'The next children will be truly yours, John.'

'These ones already are, my love. I cared for you in your pregnancy. I helped deliver them. Nothing can take that away. They are OUR children!'

John's gaze swept over the room, across the furniture that appeared more highly polished than before, the curtains and matching bedspread that seemed brighter, to rest on the bed and his beautiful wife. Her raven hair tumbled across her glowing skin as she suckled her babes. He loved her more in that moment than he had ever thought it possible to love another human being. And she was his. She and her children had come to him, and he would love them, nourish them, provide for them with every bone in his body, the best way he could till the day he died. Right now, he was the happiest man on earth. Indeed, he was the happiest man who had ever BEEN on earth.

Loath as he was to disturb the idyllic tableau, John knew that in order for Adelaide to remain comfortable he should change the sheets, give her a bed-bath and brush and comb her hair before she slept.

He was about to fetch some clean linen then he heard a loud knock echoing down the corridor from the kitchen door. Thinking it just might be evacuation orders he strode down the hallway in time to see the door open and Peter and Beatrice rush inside.

Beatrice paled when she saw John. 'Your face and arms are covered in blood! What on earth's happened?'

John looked down and grinned, 'Oh everything's just fine. Adelaide went into premature labor, but she's given birth safely and I was just about to clean up.'

Peter clapped him on the shoulder, 'Congratulations, Dad. You've beaten us all to it. What is it, boy or girl?'

'Boys.'

'What?'

'You heard. Go into the parlor, fix us all a drink, I'll clean up, and then you can come and see my family'

When John had bathed Adelaide, changed the sheets and brushed and combed her hair, he called Beatrice who was dying to see Adelaide and her new brood.

As soon as the two men were out of Adelaide's ear-shot, Peter took John aside. 'John, we're evacuating. That's what took us so long to get here. The Headman came to tell us.'

''Strewth, when?'

'The ships are on the way now. Are you prepared?'

''Course. It's better now than six hours ago. Then it could have been tricky.'

'It could still be tricky. The eruption's expected to be a big one. And it could happen at any time.'

'When do we go down to the Thunder Bay?'

'Not yet. The nearest ship's two days' sailing away. We'll have to pray, that's all.'

'I don't think it's a good idea to tell Adelaide just yet,' said John. 'We'll let her enjoy the children without worry for as long as she can.'

'I agree. And while we're talking John, did you see the doctor about your indigestion?'

'No. I'm fairly sure I know what it is.'

'Do you?'

'Yes. Which is why I didn't see the doctor. You can keep quiet about that too.'

'Don't you think Adelaide has a right to know?'

'She's too many burdens on her plate as it is. I'll deal with it in my own time.'

CHAPTER TWENTY-SEVEN

Adelaide's recovery from the birth was rapid. Within four hours she was able to walk to the bathroom. The next day she insisted on helping Beatrice with the cooking.

There was something John, Beatrice and Peter weren't telling her. She could sense it between them as palpably as if they'd had 'secret' stamped on their foreheads. There'd been talk of an evacuation for weeks, and she didn't need anyone to tell her that the major reason Beatrice and Peter were staying with her and John was to help with the babies when the time came to leave. And that time was rapidly approaching, she knew. The air was constantly filled with the sulphuric smell of rotten eggs. In places, hot water bubbled up from the ground. But it was the absence of singing birds and whirring insects that told her more than anything else that they were headed for disaster. She had painstakingly packed family photos and the wooden train John had made for Daniel on the cart that would take them all down to Thunder Bay.

But when John had brought out his oil paintings, wrapped in sheets and told her, 'These could be your insurance, Adelaide,' she'd known they were in deep trouble. Maybe deeper trouble than even the evacuation warranted.

Later, replaying the scene in her mind she could see clearly what had been wrong. Around John's lips was a thin blue line, with tiny beads of sweat sheening his brow. Fool that she was, so wrapped in the cozy, self-congratulatory warmth that came with giving birth, she'd noticed John's ashen face only subliminally, not sufficiently to remark upon it.

She'd also been wrapped up in thoughts of Luke. Her soul-mate. He would always be first in her heart, she couldn't help that any more than she could turn back the tide.

But she could look out for John. John who deserved someone to love him in a way she never could. She'd look out for him by supporting him emotionally. She hoped they'd go to South Africa, rather than England, where James Rawtenstall could hunt her down. But if they had to go to England, she'd stand up to her father-in-law and defend her own, the way John had supported and defended her.

And the plans she'd had with Danny —well, she could have more plans with John, couldn't she? He'd been looking older, more stooped recently, but she had youth and vitality on her side. John was good with children. She could start a business while John looked after the home and children. That would be far less stress on him, wouldn't it?

The baby boys were two days old when John took Adelaide aside from Beatrice and Peter. From his ashen face she knew immediately something was very wrong. Something she could never be able to put right.

'How long will it take you to pack?' he asked. 'We're evacuating. Now. The whole island.'

* * * * *

They were so well prepared all it took was for John and Peter to help Adelaide, Beatrice, the babies and Daniel into the cart, and with the horse pulling it, they set off along the steep and rocky track towards Thunder Bay.

As the horse drew to a halt on the rocky beach, John helped Adelaide step down from the cart. The ocean was calm. Too calm for her liking. A shudder tore through her body. The seaweed that lay like a protective cloak on the island had diminished.

Adelaide gazed around at the devastation wrought over the last few days. What had once been a picturesque beach, a study in the beauty and savagery of nature, was now covered by a thick layer of volcanic ash. The fertile patches of velvet grass at the tops of the cliffs, the beauty and majesty that had so enchanted her during her time here was gone. In its place was desolation. At the near end of the beach and leading into the deeper waters was a hastily erected jetty.

Instead of time standing still for Adelaide, as it usually did in periods of great stress, it speeded up. The ship that had been in the middle distance when they arrived at the beach was now docking at the end of the pier. A steady stream of passengers, men, women and children, were waiting to board. Judging by the size of the boat, not everyone would be able to get on, she knew. At the front of the line the headman, a megaphone in his hand, was addressing his people. The wind blew his words away before she could understand them. But she comprehended what he must have said when she saw the men retreating, staying only to assist the women and children on board.

John took Adelaide, a twin in each arm, Daniel clutching onto her skirts, and led her along the pier.

'Go now. I'll catch up with you later.'

'My place is with you.'

From behind them Beatrice picked up Daniel, held him in her arms. 'Hurry up, Adelaide. There's no more time. We have to go now, so the next boat can come for the men.'

Adelaide looked around. It had all happened so quickly. She hadn't had time to say goodbye. Not a proper goodbye. Not a spiritual goodbye. She hadn't had time to offer thanks for the goodness she'd received here, the charity, the compassion. The sanctuary. She'd grown to love this place. And John. It was his home, his livelihood and his inheritance. It was her children's inheritance, too.

'Hurry up, Adelaide,' repeated Beatrice behind her.

With the clarity of a thunderclap, Adelaide's mind was made up. She turned to Beatrice.

'No. I belong here.'

'What are you thinking of?'

'My children, Beatrice. My children and John.'

'John wants you on the boat.'

'If I get on that boat, and John doesn't make it, what do I tell my children about their father?'

'You tell them the truth, Adelaide. That's all.'

'I can't possibly get on that boat without John.'

'John put you and your children first. Are you going to jeopardize all that, throw it back in his face?'

'What do you mean?'

'Adelaide, I've seen you through Luke. I've seen you through John. I guessed the parentage of your children, who the twins' father is. I didn't need to be a professor to do that.'

Adelaide didn't reply. How could Beatrice have known? And if she knew, who else knew?

Beatrice tried again. 'For your children's sake, get on that boat!'

She couldn't. Much as she loved her children, much as she'd loved Luke, she couldn't leave John. Not in his hour of greatest need.

'I can't, Beatrice. I owe too much to John.'

'But you don't love him, do you?'

'In a way, yes. Very much. But not in the way he deserved to be loved.'

Beneath their feet the ground rumbled again, ominous, threatening.

'And what about the way you need to be loved, Adelaide?'

'Don't,' she begged. She'd fall apart if she thought of Luke. Even of Danny. John was her husband now. She loved him in the best way she knew how. She simply couldn't do any more.

'Your safety and your children's safety depends on your getting on that boat.'

Adelaide was afraid. Very afraid. Afraid of what would surely happen if she stayed. Even more afraid of how she would live with herself if she left. But there was some truth in what Beatrice was saying. She couldn't afford to lose her children. She'd always put them first, which was why she'd come to Damnation Island in the first place. To provide a place of safety for Daniel.

Luke.

She'd lost him because of the mess her life had been. If she got on the boat now, she could take her children once more to safety. Behind her the mountain spewed rock particles and sulphur. How would she explain John to them when they were older? How could she explain leaving him in his darkest hour?

She removed her foot from the gangplank.

'Beatrice, I've done enough running. I'm not going anywhere without John.'

'Adelaide, how would Luke feel if he knew?'

Adelaide didn't hesitate. She looked her friend levelly in the eye. 'He'd tell me to follow my conscience and do what's right. There would be no two ways about that.'

'Then I'll stay with you.'

The two young women, their arms full of babies, turned away from the boat, away from safety, towards their husbands and certain death.

CHAPTER TWENTY-EIGHT

On the beach, a gruff silence fell upon the small remaining group of people as they watched the SS *Springbok* steam away to safety. The group comprised mainly men, Adelaide and Beatrice, the only young women, though a couple of older women had also stayed. These women, their faces lined with the signatures of years of outside work had also arrived here in their youths as mail-order brides. Adelaide knew them slightly. They helped their husbands clear the already clean jetty as they waited. The younger men set together as one, hefting rocks from the beach, building a shelter lest the next ship should be unavoidably detained. John worked with them, directing a rock here, placing another rock there, pulling them together into a team. The padre and the women pulled out their rosary beads and began to pray, a low chanting rhythm, to help the men work.

Aside from the prayers, no-one spoke. To have done so, Adelaide knew, would be to have broken faith. The faith that was keeping them courageous. They all knew what their fates would be if the second ship didn't arrive. Or if it arrived too late. Any shelter they built would be effective only as a spiritual one, rather than a physical one.

Finally John spoke. 'Adelaide, you need to be on the ship.'

'No John, my place is with you. We'll always be together. I'm your wife.'

Beneath their stout shoes the ground rumbled and shifted. At

Adelaide's feet a small fissure opened in the ground and a jet of foul-smelling steam geyser upwards. Holding her babies tightly to her breast, she backed away. From the top of the mountain came sparks of crimson fire, bringing with it thick ash, reducing visibility to feet instead of miles. Around her, her neighbors spluttered and choked on the foul air.

When the walls were erected, fern fronds were placed across the tops to form a roof. Three of the younger men ran into the ocean, stroking powerfully towards the layer of seaweed that surrounded the island, returning with thick strands of it to place across the top of the fern-roof. Finally the building was complete. From the corner of her eye, Adelaide saw the headman nod slightly to the padre, who then led the entire group in prayer. They were praying, Adelaide knew, not only for deliverance, but also for the strength and courage to face what lay ahead of them.

As their prayers ended and the padre rose to his feet to bless them all, far in the distance, unmistakably, came the mournful, joyous sounds of a ship's hooter.

As one they rose, collected their belongings, and undertook the brief walk to the jetty.

Unlike the boarding of the ship in England, this one was hurried, people rushing to escape their fate. Almost too soon it was Adelaide's turn. There were no tickets to be checked this time. No goodbyes to friends and relatives waving on the quay. Not even time for a proper spiritual goodbye. This was a full retreat before the wrath of the gods. Within minutes all souls were aboard and ushered below decks to the waiting cabins.

* * * * *

Twelve minutes after reaching its destination, the boat pulled away from the tiny smoking island with its makeshift jetty. Beneath Adelaide's feet the comforting thrum of the engines, so different from the volcanic rumbles of the island, throttling up to full speed, headed out into the vast, inhospitable grayness of the South Atlantic Ocean.

She stood alone on the deck, whispering a quiet farewell to her sanctuary. This was where John had asked her to be. To say his goodbye for him. Ashen-faced and shaking he'd been unable to say farewell himself, had begged Adelaide to return to the cabin when the island was no longer in sight. It had been a strained, dignified request, and she'd had no hesitation in granting it. As the island grew smaller before her eyes, she offered silent thanks for all the good things she'd received there, the warm welcome from John, safety for herself and Daniel, John's quiet acceptance of all her children, the friendship of Beatrice and Peter. And thanks that they'd all got off the island safely.

One by one, other people arrived on deck to join her in her silent vigil at the ship's rails. No-one spoke as lava spewed from the cone of the island, to slide slowly down the mountain-side, wending its treacherous way towards the settlement, their homes and their livelihood.

A few wept silent tears, some stared fixedly, all of them stoic in their shock and grief.

* * * * *

Adelaide's emotions were in turmoil. She was relieved they were on the boat steaming towards safety. But she grieved with the islanders for their loss, for it was her loss, too. Other emotions and thoughts surfaced. Emotions she'd imagined she'd dealt with. Or at least learned to live with. The emotion of meeting, loving and leaving Luke. Back they all flooded in cinemascope. They walked as easily across her vision as waiters with silver trays filled with canapés could walk through a cocktail party —a taste here, a sample there. She didn't want to look, but was unable to turn from them. Her knuckles tightened around the ship's rail. In each frame she saw Luke, heard again his promises, his begging for a second chance, the picture he'd drawn with words of their life together. His telling her they'd travel the world together. Most of all, she heard him say he'd return for her. That could never happen now.

CHAPTER TWENTY-NINE

Hopelessly she closed her eyes against the assault.

'I was right, wasn't I?'

She screwed her eyes tighter against the hallucination, against the tactile sense of his warm breath once more fanning her neck, against the auditory hallucination of him once again whispering words of love into her ear, against the olfactory sense of his masculine scent, against the elusive sixth sense that told her he was near, that they were two equal parts of the same whole. She needed, more than anything else to reach out and touch him, feel his flesh against hers. But she couldn't, mustn't indulge in this fantasy. She owed too much to John. And besides, Luke wasn't really there, couldn't be there. A tiny part inside her died.

'I told you, my dearest beloved, do what's right, and you'll be taken care of. Always.'

She clapped her hands to her ears in an attempt to shut out the wicked hallucination. Oh, life could be so dreadfully cruel.

'I said I'd be back.'

Her eyes flew open as she whirled around. Her heart jumped joyously to her throat, her hands to her mouth. Luke! This was no hallucination. He really was here! His strongly virile form, devastating smile and calm assurance were exactly as she remembered. She put out a hand to touch him and quickly drew it back. If she touched him, she'd be lost. Hastily she looked away. She'd imagined these past few months she'd come to accept him as not being part of her life. Thought she could live without him. Deceived herself into imagining she could build a life with someone else.

She now knew she'd been appallingly, cataclysmically wrong. Without Luke there could be no life for her. She could operate on autopilot, with some days better than others, as she'd done since her arrival on Damnation Island. She could enjoy some form of intellectual life as a safety valve to stop her falling apart, as she'd also done on Damnation Island. She could even, for brief periods, fool others into thinking she was content. But she'd never, ever, be the same person without Luke. And now it was too late. Not just for her and Luke, but also for John Maggott. Too much water had passed under the bridge. For all of them.

'I told you I'd keep my promise and come back for you, Adelaide. Just in time by the looks of things.' He pointed to the smoldering island. A stream of lava was hurrying past the settlement, to the cottages. Adelaide watched, horrified, as the home she'd shared with John was swallowed, in the blinking of an eye, into the savage inferno.

She struggled not to cry out. For herself, for Luke and for John. Finally she could speak. 'No, Luke.'

He took her in his arms, 'Yes, Adelaide.' It was as if nothing had ever separated them. Not time. Not recent events. 'I took 'no' from you once before. Despite what you may have thought at the time, I never intended it to be for good.'

'We've moved on, Luke.' How she pushed the words through her lips she would never know. 'I've got to go below decks.' To John.

'Beatrice is taking care of things. You're going to listen to what I have to say if it's the last thing you do.'

If she stayed with him any longer, smelling his muskiness, feeling his closeness, she'd be ruined.

'When I was offered the job by James Rawtenstall, I couldn't see any reason not to take it on. Sure, he had a bad reputation. My mother and sisters live in one of his cottages and work in one of his mills. There was an element of coercion in the job to begin with. But the money he offered was good. So I took it.'

'You're no better than a mercenary soldier!'

'Hear me out, Adelaide.' He hesitated. 'I beg you. Listen to what I have to say. Make your decision when you've heard the full story. Please. If you still don't want me, I'll go away. But this is the only time I'll beg. You know what the right decision is. It's up to you to make it.'

She struggled. She wanted to be in his arms forever. But it was too late to turn back the clock. Wasn't it? If she listened she might hear something to make any semblance of life without him impossible. On the other hand, there could well be a flaw in his story that would give her strength to walk away from him forever. She fought with herself, was almost strong enough to say she didn't want to hear. But she was weak. She gave in. And listened.

'At first it was just a job. A well-paid one. The money he offered would pay for my sisters' education and mean my mother could take on an easier job and have a secure roof over her head. I had to ascertain whether or not you were going to Damnation Island, and if you were, I was to persuade you by whatever means to return to England. If I couldn't do that, I was to let him know your whereabouts. It was my decision, not his, to put you in that cabin on the way out. I recognized you by the mole on your cheek and on Daniel's cheek. The moment I set eyes on you, I knew somehow James Rawtenstall had got things wrong.' He held up his hand to stop her interrupting then continued. 'I don't know what it was, second sight, instinct, I just knew he was wrong. When I asked you to marry me, I was sincere. I simply didn't know how to tell you I'd been working for him. I thought, stupidly, that you'd understand. We all make mistakes,' he said with a trace of bitterness as he looked away.

When he turned back to her, his eyes were clear. 'When I received the telegram, the one you read, I didn't have time to explain things. There was an emergency elsewhere on the ship, and when I returned it was too late. You'd read it, and your mind was made up. I knew you'd been through a tremendous ordeal, losing Danny and having trouble with the Rawtenstalls, and the last thing I wanted to do was add to your troubles. I didn't want to break you, Adelaide, so I let you go.' He paused. 'I did what I thought was right at the time.'

'It might have been right at the time. But it isn't right now! Stay away from me, Luke.'

'Not till you've heard the rest. And listen you will!'

Adelaide drew in a deep breath. 'Finish it then.'

'It was obvious you'd been let down by too many people. You couldn't trust anyone. Asking you to trust me, on words alone, would have been asking too much. Actions, not words were needed. So I let you go. But not without making sure you'd be well looked after first. I spoke with the padre. He assured me there was plenty of time before the official island wedding, for me to return to England, do what I had to do and return to claim you.'

'And what did you do, Luke?' she asked flatly, trying to keep her voice steady, trying to stop her heart hammering in her chest.

Adelaide wanted to know and at the same time, couldn't bear to listen. They'd been so close to joy and happiness, and now it was impossible. How could she tell him she'd put duty before love and married John Maggott. She'd compromised her soul; she'd known that at the time. She'd married John for a name for her babies. She'd accepted his shelter, taken his love. And he did love her, she knew that. He'd just lost his home and his livelihood. John needed her now. She could never live with herself if she let him down. The dilemma was impossible. Whichever way she went now, she would always be torn in two. She had John's love and forgiveness on one hand and the love of her life and her soul-mate on the other, the man she couldn't live without. Surely death would be easier than this. There would be no further chances with Luke, she knew. And that was all she'd wanted. All they'd both wanted. A second chance at happiness. Was it all that much to ask? Luke's words of several months earlier came back with alarming clarity. 'If we do the right thing, everything will turn out fine, you'll see.' to mock them all and their dreadful situation. If only Luke had returned to Damnation Island before the shakes began, before the eruption, things might well have worked out. John would have been able to carry on his life as before. Saddened for a while, no doubt. If there had been no eruption he would have had his home, friends, livelihood. Now, he would have nothing.

Slowly, despairingly she turned to Luke, her soul's passion, the love of her life. 'It's too late, Luke.'

He took her shoulders in his hands, forcing her eyes to meet his. 'What are you afraid of, Adelaide? Your own emotions? I don't think so. You still wear my pendant around your neck. We're going to be married!'

'I'm already married.' she said flatly.

'By proxy only! Look in my eyes and tell me you love him Adelaide. Tell me you love him more than me.'

'I can't...' If she did...she couldn't, wouldn't entertain the thought. She looked away.

Luke took her by the shoulders, shaking them. 'Tell me, Adelaide. Tell me you love him more than me. Then I'll leave you alone for the rest of eternity!'

Adelaide felt her eyes fill with tears, felt her skin moisten as they rolled unchecked down her cheeks. She remained silent, not trusting herself to speak.

'Of course you can't. Before this ship reaches port we'll be married.'

This was what she wanted. What she'd always wanted. 'The marriage can't be annulled!'

'If I fill your belly full of babies it can!'

She mustn't tell him he'd already done that. If he knew, what difference would that make —to them all? He mustn't find out. If he did, he'd confront John. She couldn't allow that to happen to either of them.

'I repeat, it can't be annulled!' she said, then softer, 'John and I have already undergone a civil ceremony.'

Luke's face hardened. 'You didn't wait long, did you?' he mocked. 'I've been away in England, dealing to James Rawtenstall, knocking some sense into the man. Do you realize I've been in prison for you, while all the time you languished in another man's arms? Well, I'm back to claim what's mine.'

He gathered her into his embrace, holding her fiercely. 'I'm going to make sure you never forget who loved you first. Who always loved you. I'll fill your belly with children, no matter who you imagine you're married to. Every one of them will look like me, like both of us. I'll defy anyone, for whatever reason, to keep us apart!'

Desperate, the fraction of her mind that could still think tried to escape, while her body fought to surrender. Heaven forbid John should find her in this position.

'Luke, if you truly love me, I beg of you listen to what I have to say.'

'Oh, I'll listen, my lovely,' he purred. 'I'll listen while you beg me to take you again and again like we did before. And while you're thinking of a way to beg me, you can remember how much I loved you. How much I still love you. There's no other woman for me, Adelaide. And no other man for you. I went back to England on your behalf. The Headman told me the legal ceremony wouldn't take place for twelve months. I evened things out, man to man, with James Rawtenstall. You can be a free women legally, Adelaide.'

'Legally, maybe.'

His hands roamed her waist, the flare of her hips, her thighs, 'What other way is there? Don't tell me you don't love me. I know how you responded the first time. How you want to respond now. We're soul-mates. You know that as well as I do. We complete each other. Two halves of the same whole.'

'What you're saying is true, Luke. But there's something you don't know,' she gasped.

'Try me.' His voice hardened again.

'When I first set foot on Damnation Island I was pregnant. I didn't know it at the time. I wasn't pregnant when I first set foot on the ship, and there was no one else but you.'

He stopped what he was doing, looking at her in amazement. 'You're not pregnant now —what happened?' His eyes narrowed, 'You didn't...surely?'

'No, Luke. I was very sick. Sicker than I've ever been in my entire life. John was the kindest man you could ever hope to meet. He arranged a swift wedding so the baby would have a father and people wouldn't talk.'

'By my reckoning you should be heavily pregnant by now.'

'Yes Luke, I should be.'

'So what happened?' he asked tonelessly.

'I went into labor early.'

Luke's anger gave way to shock. 'Oh, my dearest, what happened to our baby?'

'They're in the cabin. With Beatrice and John.' That was it. Out now. God help her.

'Was it a boy or a girl?'

'Boys.'

'Boys?'

'I had twins, Luke. I now have three sons, Daniel, Luke and John.'

'I'm going to see my sons.'

My sons. He'd said it. They were his. He had a right to see them. She wanted him to see them. But not at the price of John's peace of mind.

'Luke, I listened to you talk about letting me go when we reached Damnation Island. I heard you out. Will you hear me out, too?'

'It'd better be good!'

'Neither of us could have known at the time, but if you had to commit me and our children to someone's care, you couldn't have chosen a better man than John Maggott. In the decency stakes he's second to none. He accepted Daniel, along with me. I didn't tell him about you. I wanted that part of my life...sacred. He undertook not to consummate our union until we were legally married, so I could have time to think through my life and what I wanted to do. He provided everything he could for me.'

Luke interrupted. 'Were you happy with him?'

'Luke, you were the love of my life. Nothing compared nor ever could with that.'

'Were you happy?'

'I plodded on, as best I could, from day to day. He treated me well.'

Luke's eyes narrowed, his head inclined slightly. Adelaide continued. 'John asked me if I was pregnant when I became sick. I reassured him that I wasn't. Of course, several days later I had to tell him that I was, after all, pregnant. He arranged a civil marriage so the babies wouldn't be illegitimate. He delivered them. He's twice my age, Luke. He's lost his home, his livelihood. If I desert him now, I'll never be able to live with myself.'

'Will you answer two questions, Adelaide?'

'Yes.'

'Do you love me?' His hair flamed back from his face as he held her tightly, holding her gaze with his.

'Oh, Luke, how can you even ask?' Adelaide met his gaze firmly, wanting to be held in his arms forever, knowing that was not possible.

'Do you love me?' he demanded.

'I've dreamt of you every single night. Every day I've hoped you'd return. When I've been stuck with a difficult decision, I've asked myself, 'What would Luke do?' She struggled in his arms and broke loose from his embrace. 'Of course I love you!'

'Thank you. Do you love John Maggott?'

Adelaide looked away from Luke. 'Not in the way he deserves to be loved. I like and respect him. I'm loyal to him. I can't do any more.'

Luke took her in his arms once more. 'Adelaide, I did what I thought was best for you when you were going to Damnation Island. I didn't see any other honorable way. Given the same set of circumstances, knowing what I do now, it would have been wiser not to let you go to Damnation. Here we are again, with different circumstances, but the choice is the same, love or honor?'

'It has to be honor, Luke.' Adelaide felt a sob rise in her throat. 'As you yourself said, 'If we do what's right, we won't miss out.'

Tears started again from the corners of her eyes. 'On the way to Damnation I thought it right to put duty first. It wasn't easy. This is far, far harder, but I cannot let John down, not when he needs me.' The tears coursed unchecked down her cheeks. Uncaring of how it looked, she dashed them away with her fist. 'Can you understand that?'

'Can you understand what I went through in England for you?' Luke's tone was almost pleading.

'I think so.' This was the hardest thing she'd ever had to do. 'But I'm married to John and that's the way it's going to stay.'

'Then this is goodbye, Adelaide.' Luke's face was anguished, his tone filled with sadness. 'I won't see our sons now. It's better that way. For all of us. Take care of them.' He released her from his embrace, turned to go and stopped. 'Before I go, tell me why you still wear my pendant?'

'That's a measure of how good John is. He could have sawn it off —I asked him to. He said you were part of my history, and I should keep it on. He's also the one who named our second son Luke, so both boys could be proud of their natural father.'

'I see,' said Luke, his voice ragged.

Then he was gone, leaving Adelaide alone with the wind, the waves and the muffled sounds of explosions from Damnation Island, as it began to disappear into the distance.

CHAPTER THIRTY

As she opened the door to her cabin, the silence hit her like a thunderclap. This wasn't just the aftermath of Luke, of a soul bereft of its mate. It was much more. She looked around. Daniel and the little twins were sleeping silently in their cots. John was asleep on the double bed, his face ashen, his features haggard. Icy tentacles of fear gripped Adelaide's heart. John opened his eyes, gazed fixedly, then when his eyes fell upon Adelaide his focus cleared, and he smiled. A return smile eased through her own lips. Slowly John sat up. 'Just a touch of indigestion. Let's go on deck, shall we? I could do with some fresh air.'

Gently, with infinite tenderness, Adelaide helped John out of bed and up the steep steps to the deck. The day was like a funeral shroud, grey with volcanic ash, rent occasionally by pyrotechnic flashes that illuminated the devastated island in the distance. She watched in horrified fascination as the home they'd shared was engulfed by the inferno. In the blinking of an eye, everything John held dear was ravaged. Adelaide could have wept for him.

As the ship steered its passengers to safety, an older woman standing nearby sobbed into her handkerchief. John went up to her, and putting his arms around her heaving shoulders, comforted her as Adelaide watched. Slowly the woman's sobs subsided, and she went below decks, leaving John and Adelaide alone together.

John put his hand to his pocket. 'This letter's for you. It came by telegraph when the twins were being born. Keep it. The original can't arrive now. It's from a solicitor in Manchester.'

Adelaide looked at John, at his face now ashen, older-looking. He continued. 'I had to read it. I wasn't sure it was for you at first. When I did know, I didn't know how to tell you.' Adelaide watched with concern as his lips took on a bluish tinge, his breathing became a series of gasps. She didn't want to take the envelope. He thrust it into her hands. 'Take it, Adelaide. There's nothing in it to hurt you. Read it later if you wish, but promise me you won't destroy it.'

Solemnly she took the envelope. 'I promise.'

Then she opened the envelope and took out the single sheet of paper.

'Confirm paintings worth $10,000. Letter to follow in the mail.

From the Rochester Gallery, Manchester.'

She turned to John.

'I told you your paintings were good..'

John cut her off,

'Adelaide, there's something you need to know about me...just in case anything happens...'

'John, I'm sure...'

'Hear me out. Please. It's for your own good. I've taken great pride in my physical strength and agility, despite my looks. But I've had to make the most of things. I don't really suffer from indigestion, Adelaide. I've known what it was for years. I've got a weak heart. Oh, I've never let it stand in the way of doing what I wanted. But I feel time's running out. If I don't survive this trip, take my paintings and sell them. You'll understand when you read the contents of the envelope. There will be enough money to support you and the children, if you have to.'

'John, I...'

'Wait. I'd rather you weren't alone. You need a man in your bed, Adelaide, someone to warm the sheets at night. Promise me you won't waste your time grieving.'

'You're justifiably upset at losing your home. But you're not going to die, John.'

He smiled weakly. 'Sometime, dearest, we've all got to go. All I ask is that you heed my words. I wouldn't have missed one single moment of our life together.' He clutched his chest and leaned forward as another spasm of pain gripped him, causing him to collapse, convulsing to the deck. A thin film of sweat beaded his brow, his convulsions slowed, ceased and he lay unconscious. Adelaide knelt by his side, knowing in her heart, that this was the end. And she had wasted their final hour together arguing with Luke.

The veil of sorrow fell heavily upon her shoulders, rendering her unaware of anyone at her side, except for the dim knowledge that a familiar hand was reaching out to touch John, search for his pulse. Luke's voice was in her ears, whispering urgently. 'Adelaide, tell him what you need to. Now.'

John's eyes fluttered open. 'Adelaide,' he gasped. 'Find the twins' father. Let him see his children.' He stopped as pain wracked him again, then continued. 'You've brought me joy and happiness like I never believed was possible. You've been good to me, even though your heart was elsewhere. I can die a happy man, dearest, if you promise me you'll marry the children's father.'

'She promises,' said Luke.

John turned to Luke. 'As soon as I saw you when we came aboard I knew it was you. Make sure she sells my paintings. I want you both to benefit from them.'

He closed his eyes, took in a breath. It didn't come back out. Luke put his fingers on John's eyes and gently closed them.

* * * * *

Hours later, as the sun was setting, crew and passengers alike stood on deck as John's body was committed to the Deep. Everyone grieved, Adelaide, the inhabitants of Damnation, the crew who'd only just met him. Luke kept a respectful silence.

Adelaide knew she'd miss him, more than she could ever say. She never would have the chance to repay his kindness to her. She couldn't have repaid it if she'd lived to be a hundred. As these thoughts swirled about her head, Arthur Glass, the Headman, stepped forward.

'This is John's last will, dictated to me and witnessed by the padre and the ship's Captain as we boarded.

'I, John Maggott, being of sound mind and sick body, bequeath all my worldly possessions to my wife, Adelaide. If I should die before we reach safety I want Adelaide to marry the father of her children, Luke Collins, who I have discovered is a crew member of this ship. Adelaide and I shared a wonderful, happy marriage. She brought me untold joy. However, her heart belongs, as it always has, to Luke. I was merely the temporary custodian of it and was happy in that role. I've known for many years that my days have been numbered. I owe Adelaide a great debt of gratitude for the joy she has brought into my life. I hope you will all join me in supporting, with love, my wife and her new husband.

God Bless,

John Maggott.

EPILOGUE

Lucia Fitzgerald sat on her bed, fingering the thick envelope carefully, her tired eyes taking in the painstakingly inscribed letters on the front. Her grandmother's handwriting. She'd know those careful, sloping letters anywhere.

She hesitated, not wanting to open it, knowing in her heart it was goodbye, knowing that eventually she'd resist the temptation and would have to open it. But not just yet. She sighed. Her grandmother had always possessed an uncanny ability to gaze into her soul, to know what she was planning, to understand all she was thinking. And Lucia had never minded. Until now.

Her fingers crept around the edges of the envelope. Whatever was inside seemed like a gift, wrapped in layer upon layer of soft paper. And the rest was a thick wad of paper. Could the old lady really know what she was planning?

A shudder shook through her young body. She hoped the old lady didn't know. The last thing Lucia wanted to do was to hurt the woman she'd come to admire, respect and cherish.

Her fingers traced the bottom on the envelope, found a hidden something hard and unyielding, beneath them.

Unable to resist any longer she tore open the envelope and pulled out the leaves of paper. Onto the carpet by her feet slipped a small package.

Lucia leaned forward from her bed, retrieved the package and held it in her hand as she began to read the letter.

High Castle Craggs
14 November 2004

My dear Lucia,

You have a good heart, but possess a willful, headstrong streak. That is why this sealed package is for you. The gift is ancient, valuable beyond price.

You see, I know you're planning to elope. It was your restlessness and secrecy that alerted me to what, if I'm honest, I've always known you would one day consider. I, too, married young and now it is your turn. I wish you nothing but joy and pleasure, although I do know that life will bring its challenges for you. Still, I believe you'll overcome and gain strength from them, as I did. First of all you need to read the long sheaf of paper I have enclosed for you. It is my story, and I hope it will serve as a guide for you. It's my life, and it seems like your life is going to emulate mine.

This morning when the letter with the overseas postmark arrived, my suspicions were confirmed. Surprised, my dear? Don't be. Lucia, when you look at me you see withered skin and wrinkled eyes. But the same blood that once coursed through my veins now courses through yours. I'm not hurt by your decision. I know you will do what's best. And in the long run that's all that counts. What I'm about to tell you is true. We're of the same blood, you and I.

Emeralds, Lucia. Folk say they're like pearls and opals, that they bring tears and sadness to the wearer. That's pure rubbish. Life and loving bring tears. That's fact, not silly superstition. Loving also brings its rewards, and that's not rubbish either!

The other facts you need to know about this pendant are that I've worn it for over fifty years, never once taking it off. It was very old when it was given to me and had been passed down through generation upon generation of the women in our family.

You've a decision to make, and it won't be easy. They never are. However, what I have just shared with you may well help. Whatever your decision, the emerald is yours to keep.

Whenever life becomes tough, clasp your fingers around it. Feel its warmth as I did. Be comforted as I was.

You're just heard most of my story. Now hear the rest.

Four months after John's death, Luke, Daniel, Luke Junior, John Junior and I arrived back in England. After a decent interval Luke and I were legally married. Spiritually, we'd always been married.

But we weren't married until, at Luke's insistence, a memorial service for John had been held. It was important to Luke that his extended family and friends pay homage to the man who had cared for me and our children. John was buried at sea, as is the custom. You recall the Damnation Forest on the south of the property? That's for the memory of John, where his spirit can rest among the native trees, facing south, in the direction of Damnation.

John and I had two more children, twins again, girls this time. Adelaide he named after me, and Joanna, your mother, in John's memory.

And that is the story of our journey to High Castle Craggs.

It's a story of a great love found, lost and regained. A story that tells of different loves, different passions. Of faith, great hope and even greater charity.

There's a lesson to be learned. As Luke, your grandfather said, 'Do what's right and you'll be okay.' And as grandfather John said, 'We do the best we can. That's all.'

We find love in unexpected places, at unexpected times. It's not always the love we recognize, but if we do what's right, love and our soul-mate will find us.

Wear the emerald pendant, Lucia. Rejoice in its story. Love and be happy.

From your loving grandmother,
Adelaide

THE END

Beth Heywood

Beth Heywood lives with her husband in a large book-filled home in a remote and lonely farming outpost on New Zealand's North Island, which they share with two large dogs, Bram and Stoker. The neighbouring population is made up of farmers, potters, artists and shark and marlin fishermen, all of which is conducive to good writing.

Beth is an avid reader of romance and horror and has taught Creative Writing for several years. She has had short stories and poetry published under the name of Liz Heywood.

Beth is currently at work on her next novel.

Printed in the United States
201987BV00002B/154-210/P

9 781934 041598